W9-API-147

Miriam's destiny is marriage and motherhood. Not tracking down a thief who stole the scrolls containing the Alchemical League's most valuable formulas

Miriam bat Isaac is a budding alchemist in first-century CE Alexandria. Who in her household or among her Shabbat guests stole the scrolls with her occult secrets? Was it her frantic father, on the cusp of financial ruin, eager for Miriam to end her dalliance and marry into an honorable and wealthy family? Her rebellious brother, intent on raising the money to travel to Capua so he can enroll in the Roman Empire's most renowned gladiator school? Or her faint-hearted fiancé, who begrudges her preoccupation with alchemy and yearns for their forthcoming marriage?

And how did the thief manage to steal them? Miriam is not only faced with a baffling puzzle, but to recover the scrolls, she must stalk the culprit through the sinister alleys of Alexandria's claustrophobic underbelly. The Romans who occupy her city are trouble enough.

The Deadliest Lie

by

June Trop

Bell Bridge Books

This is a work of fiction. Names, characters, places and incidents are either the products of the author's imagination or are used fictitiously. Any resemblance to actual persons (living or dead), events or locations is entirely coincidental.

Bell Bridge Books
PO BOX 300921
Memphis, TN 38130
Print ISBN: 978-1-61194-367-2

Bell Bridge Books is an Imprint of BelleBooks, Inc.

Copyright © 2013 by June Trop Zuckerman

Printed and bound in the United States of America.

All rights reserved. No part of this book may be reproduced in any form or by any electronic or mechanical means, including information storage and retrieval systems, without permission in writing from the publisher, except by a reviewer, who may quote brief passages in a review.

We at BelleBooks enjoy hearing from readers.
Visit our websites – www.BelleBooks.com and www.BellBridgeBooks.com.

10 9 8 7 6 5 4 3 2 1

Cover design: Debra Dixon
Interior design: Hank Smith
Photo/Art credits:
Hieroglyphs (manipulated) © Diego Elorza | Dreamstime.com
Pharos Lightouse (manipulated) © George Bailey | Dreamstime.com
Woman and columns (manipulated) © Algol | Dreamstime.com
Gold texture (manipulated) © Wyoosumran | Dreamstime.com

:Lldc:01:

Dedication

In memory of my parents,
Esther Charlotte Gittleman Trop and Nathan Trop

THE HOME OF
MIRIAM BAT ISAAC
THE YEAR 46 CE -ALEXANDRIA

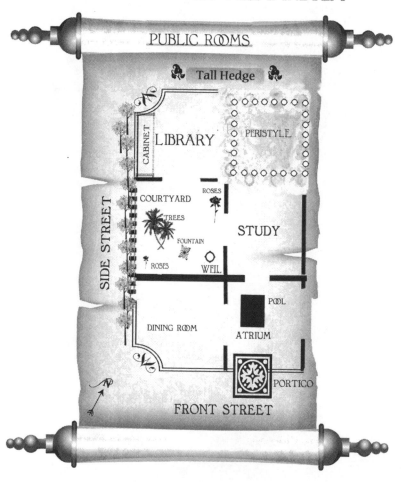

PUBLIC ROOMS

Tall Hedge

LIBRARY

CABINET

PERISTYLE

SIDE STREET

COURTYARD

TREES

ROSES

FOUNTAIN

ROSES

WELL

STUDY

DINING ROOM

POOL

ATRIUM

PORTICO

FRONT STREET

"Bread of falsehood is sweet to a man, but afterwards his mouth shall be filled with gravel."
—*Proverbs* 20:17

Summer of the Sixth Year of the Reign of
Tiberius Claudius Caesar Augustus
Germanicus [Claudius]

46 CE

Alexandria *ad Aegyptum*

Chapter 1

Late Friday Afternoon

I WONDERED WHAT lie I'd tell as I approached the great mahogany doors of my father, Isaac ben Asher's study. By this evening, the beginning of *Shabbat*, I was to have fixed on the date of my marriage to my dearest friend, the childhood companion I'd been betrothed to since infancy. My father was increasingly impatient for me to marry Noah, the only son of his business partner, Amram ben Eleazar, and thereby secure the future of our families.

His study is a small square room off the atrium, perfumed by the roses in the courtyard to its west. I squared my shoulders upon entering, but as soon as I sat before his massive ebony desk and saw the set of his jaw, my shoulders curved inward.

He wasted no time.

"The date, Miriam?"

I would rather have endured a public flogging than the humiliation I felt under his gaze.

"You promised you'd give me a date so the wedding could take place before your seventeenth birthday."

The low-hanging midsummer sun streaming in from the courtyard painted a glow on his swarthy, heavy-featured face and splashed a disjointed pattern across the ledgers stacked on the shelves covering the east wall.

My head dropped in shame, and any words I might have formed got trapped somewhere between my mind and my tongue.

"Look up when I'm speaking to you, young lady."

I'd been picking at the threads of the plain short-sleeved,

ankle-length tunic of bleached linen that I wore with a thin Numidian leather belt, my usual Friday attire before bathing and dressing for *Shabbat*. When I raised my eyes, I could see that his burly shoulders had stiffened under his blue cotton tunic and the lines at the corners of his mouth had deepened into creases.

"We've made a commitment to this family, Miriam, a commitment as binding as marriage, and like marriage, it can be broken by only a divorce. Besides, Amram is not just my partner; he's my friend. We've seen each other through the worst of times, when your mother died and later when he lost his beloved Leah and their two daughters in the Pogrom."

My father cleared his throat and continued his lecture.

"You're shirking your responsibility not only to me but to our community, to say nothing of the insult and embarrassment your delay is inflicting on a fine family. Even your mother, the soul of temperance, would blanch at your indifference to duty."

My father was obsessed with his sense of duty.

The heat of the room clamped down on me despite the cool breath of the Etesian winds billowing and snapping the purple tied-back drapes that skirt the floor and separate Papa's study from the peristyle. The arrangement of our cobblestone streets takes full advantage of these salubrious northwesterly winds. Originating in the Aegean, they whisper across the Mediterranean to temper our summer sun and are the longed-for relief from the desert's Khamseen winds, the hot south winds that choke us with their suffocating walls of dust during the spring and debilitate us with headaches, deafness, and the other ailments they carry.

Looking past Papa and into the breeze, I tried to find serenity in the shade of the peristyle's lush ferns and cascading ivy and the screen of boxwoods beyond its colonnade.

"I can't understand you, Miriam. No one could be more devoted to you than Noah."

"But I'm not sure I love Noah, not like a husband, not the way you loved Mama."

He'd never stopped grieving for my mother. Following two still births, she'd become pregnant once again, this time with my twin brother Binyamin and me. After our birth, childbed fever claimed her life and any tenderness my father might have had.

"Miriam, security, not love, is the foundation of a marriage. The purpose of marriage is to preserve and extend a family's resources. Especially for Jews, given our precarious civil status, the matter of resources is crucial. When you were an infant, I agreed to the alliance with Noah's family to diversify our holdings. Love, if it comes at all, comes later. I'm counting on you to safeguard the future of our family. I'm already forty years old, and your brother is too busy ogling every prostitute that waits for a legionnaire at the Gate of the Sun."

Tears of shame trickled down my cheeks for delaying the marriage against my father's wishes. But I knew he'd never force me to marry Noah. I was his favorite, the child who grew each day to resemble the woman he had immortalized in a bronze statue, as if the sculptor could resurrect my mother from the grave. As if I could bury my face in the statue's indifferent bosom, experience the comfort of a mother's arms around me, and draw her consoling scent into my nostrils. When I was little, I would close my eyes and roll myself into a ball to imagine what my life was like inside her, and to this day I long to know her.

Papa says he sees in me the same elegance she had, from her tall slender frame, the gentle slope of her shoulders, and the graceful curve of her hairline to the delicate planes of her face, her darkly fringed eyes, narrow nose, and the cloud of luxuriant curls that framed her brow. So when I see my reflection, I wonder whether I'm also looking at her, except that my hair is chestnut, whereas hers was blonde, and my eyes are the blue of lapis lazuli, whereas Papa says hers changed color like the Mediterranean. Otherwise, he says, we're identical, that even my skin is like hers. "As smooth as silk and as translucent as Oriental alabaster," he says, except for the worry lines between my brows and my easy blush. Still, when his eyes snared mine and he pulled in a deep breath, my own lungs emptied out. I knew he was about to upbraid me.

"Don't deny it, Miriam. I know you've been spending afternoons with that bastard Judah." A stream of sour breath accompanied his bitter words. He was leaning toward me now, his thick legs flung apart, his pupils dilated, his jowls waddling as he stirred the air right under my nose with his accusing finger. "Remember who you are. You're a well-educated Jewess and a Roman citizen."

He spaced out his words as he said "a Roman citizen."

Generations ago, our family and Noah's purchased Roman citizenship, a privilege that's hereditary only when both parents are citizens. Roman citizenship guarantees redress in the Roman courts, as well as immunity from the most onerous taxes and services. Not only was Judah reared without the respectability of a father's name, but he's had no protection against tax collector greed and intimidation, which, through a single misfortune, could reduce him to poverty, even slavery.

I remember when our tinker was stabbed to death while gambling in a saloon near the waterfront. All I can recall of him now is how ill-suited he was to his name, Plato (meaning broad-shouldered). An overlong neck connected his jutting, hollow face and Adam's apple to a pair of boyish shoulders, while the rest of his gangly frame perched on hairless, spindly legs. His impoverished widow and children had to be sold to slavers when they couldn't pay the tax collector.

"You're not some waif, Miriam, eking out a pitiful living in some filthy stall in the agora."

"Papa, Papa, please. Judah is just our client. I see him only on the calends to collect his mortgage payment." My tongue crafted the lie as I stared into the eyes of the asp cut into the glass oil lamp on his desk. Had I fooled him, or had he caught that barely perceptible moment of hesitation before my answer? "I cannot commit to a wedding date today, Papa. Please, just one more week. I beg you."

When he dropped his head into his hands, I knew our meeting was over, that I would have but seven more days. Lest he change his mind, I wheeled out of the chair, nearly toppling it over, my knees stiff from the stress of our meeting, the pressure of a headache gathering across my eyes. While crossing the mosaic floor to the mahogany doors, I wiped my sticky palms on the skirt of my tunic so I could turn the bronze door handles. Counting each step to the vaulted atrium, I heard a faint whistle of relief escape my pursed lips as I circled the sunken marble pool edged with planters of white chamomiles and yellow field marigolds and passed through the archway into our dining room.

Chapter 2

Friday, Late Afternoon into Early *(Shabbat)* Evening

THE IMAGE OF frustration on Papa's face and my own shame for failing to fulfill his expectations lingered while I bathed for *Shabbat*, brushed my hair into a simple bun, and dressed in a fresh, short-sleeved white linen tunic embroidered with a blue primitive border print. Then I began to arrange the dining room for Noah and Amram to join my father, brother, Aunt Hannah, and me as they usually did for the *Shabbat* evening meal. Positioning the room's three purple dining couches in an arc facing the courtyard, I centered them around a low ivory table, its legs carved in the figure of a squatting griffin. Then, measuring the distances with my forearm to get the symmetry just right, I flanked each couch with a pair of enameled ebony lamp stands.

Frescoed streaks of purple tint the dining room's ceiling and western wall to suggest the cooling fingers of dusk and match the color of the opium poppies along the perimeter of the courtyard, their beds along the street framed by a lattice fence and, beyond the fence, a thicket of thistle and acacia. A hedge of hibiscus screens our well near the southeastern corner of the courtyard, while dwarf plane trees and date palms splash shade on the marble fountain in the center and the wrought-iron chaise lounges around it.

From the dining room, through the fountain's murmur, I could hear Aunt Hannah playing the cithara in the library, as she customarily does before *Shabbat*. Blind since birth, my father's only sibling has always lived with us. After my mother's death,

Aunt Hannah, with the help of our much-loved slave Iphigenia, reared Binyamin and me. Aunt Hannah, more a co-conspirator than a parent, encouraged us to follow our dreams as she could not. Easing her broad hips into her spindly-legged chair, she holds the cithara between her ample forearms, strumming it with a pick in her right hand and dampening its strings with her left, creating in each note a lustrous jewel. When she senses the setting sun, she ends her recital, the signal for me to light the *Shabbat* candles. Despite the lifeless chips of jade that camouflage as her eyes, Aunt Hannah sees more than most.

Papa, Noah, and Binyamin were also in the library, absorbing Aunt Hannah's melodies and sampling the wine and stuffed olives, boiled eggs, and candied almonds served in anticipation of the arrival of Amram, who was attending Philo's lecture at the Great Synagogue. Philo and his younger brother Alexander Lysimachus head our city's foremost Jewish family, one that has enjoyed wealth here for generations and the benefit of Roman citizenship since the days of Julius Caesar.

As much as Alexander Lysimachus has dedicated his life to the affairs of state, Philo has dedicated his to harmonizing Greek philosophy with the Truth of the *Torah*. Although most Jews dismiss his work as more Greek than Jewish—some deride him for turning Moses into Plato and Plato into Moses—Amram idolizes Philo for having led the embassy during the Pogrom to petition Caligula to guarantee our rights and safety. In gratitude, Amram goes to hear Philo lecture wherever and whenever he can. So we waited for him while Papa, Noah, and Binyamin snacked on the refreshments in the library.

The aromas of roast duck and grilled lamb nibbled at my stomach as I kindled the oil lamps. Then, when Aunt Hannah had ended her cadence, I used the flame from one of the lamps to melt a *Shabbat* candle into each of the two freestanding Jerusalem stone candlesticks that had been my mother's. We keep them in our dining room along the street-side windows to remind us of her holiness. Aunt Hannah taught me to light two candles, one for each of the two *Torah* commandments about our holy days: to remember them and to keep them holy. Recalling when she used to have to lift me to reach them, I beckoned their flickering light and added to the traditional blessing my own prayers for peace between Papa and me.

In the stillness of *Shabbat*, along with the chink of passing crockery and the splash of flowing wine, the cool winds off the waterfront swept the conversation in the library across the courtyard into the dining room.

"I wonder, Noah, why you didn't accompany your father to Philo's lecture." Papa was admonishing him. I could picture Noah's face turning the color of strawberries before he'd drop his head and stare at his feet.

"My father should stop living in the past. All he does is relive the Pogrom." Papa had touched on Noah's only gripe against his brokenhearted father.

The Pogrom erupted in 38 when I was eight years old. Papa said it really began when Flaccus, the Roman governor of Alexandria and prefect of Egypt, issued an edict depriving us Jews of our civil liberties and branding us aliens in the very city we'd lived in since its founding. The effect of that edict, he said, was to give free reign to the Gentiles to settle old scores against us: the Greeks, for our expanding commercial interests, our resistance to assimilation, and our seeming favoritism under Roman rule; and the Egyptians, for our unrestrained attacks against them in our literature, especially in *The Wisdom of Solomon*, where we depict them as animal-worshippers and claim their long-standing oppression is a justifiable punishment from G-d.

But I remember it starting with the fist of an explosion, when, at the beginning of *Tishri*, on our High Holy Days, mobs of Alexandrian Greeks abetted by the Egyptian rabble stormed the sanctuary of the Great Synagogue during our morning prayers. They kicked through every entrance, smashing the bejeweled doors, grinding the semiprecious stones beneath their heels, saving their clubs and swords for us. That's when Papa thrust me under our pew, and in that dry and dusty stripe of darkness I heard the world shatter and fall in a hailstorm of bricks, stones, glass, and screams.

And I saw sandaled feet: Some pale and dainty, others thick and hairy. Some veiny and caramel-colored, others leathery and loose-jointed. Even a few of dubious cleanliness. But none stood rooted. Some limped, others stumbled, but most ran helter-skelter. Until they stopped. Abruptly. There was no escape. Their feet were outnumbered by those in boots caked with grit and later with flesh and clots of blood.

That was just the prelude. By the time that horrific month was over, we had all—men, women, and children—been evicted from the other quarters of the city, herded into a narrow sector of the Jewish Quarter, and threatened with arrest and summary execution if we appeared outside that sector, even in a desperate search for food.

During the months afterward, I would see our men, now despondent, loitering on heat-drenched street corners, whispering in huddles. They'd hush when they heard me coming, but I knew what they were talking about. I'd already overheard Amram telling Papa about the crucifixion of our most senior elder, Baruch ben Ezekiel. And, as if that weren't bad enough, the rest of our elders were being dragged into the theater, where, for the amusement of the mob, they were stripped and scourged or bound to the wheel and mauled like the vilest criminals. Then the entertainment would continue with dancing and flute-playing contests.

Still other Jews had been hauled into the marketplace to be stoned, pummeled, torn limb from limb, or burned alive. Their properties were burned, their corpses were desecrated, and their women, under threat of torture, were forced to eat the flesh of swine. One night, when Noah and Amram were attending a meeting to organize an appeal to Caligula, a gang of thugs trapped Leah and the girls in their home, smashed their shutters, and hurled volleys of lit torches through their windows to set their furnishings ablaze. Then they mocked their cries as the smoke suffocated them and the hissing flames devoured them.

"Don't you think it's only right that your father remember

your mother and sisters and pay his respects to Philo?" Papa's goading Noah was useless. Noah was too tame, too morally fastidious to ever raise his voice, let alone to my father, let alone on *Shabbat*.

"Philo may fancy himself the great advocate, but he accomplished nothing for our people. All he did was truckle to Caligula, tagging along with his delegation to Caligula's seaside villa, begging for a hearing. Instead, Caligula treated the five of them like a theatrical farce. We had to wait for Claudius's ascension to have our rights reaffirmed."

I got the feeling Noah was playing to Papa's disdain for Philo more than challenging his father's admiration for him. And when he continued, I was sure of it.

"Besides, it's useless to dwell on the past. I'd rather look ahead to my marriage to Miriam and our rearing a family."

More ammunition for Papa.

After a considerable silence, I heard someone, probably Papa, open a fresh amphora of wine, dilute it with water in the crater, a two-handled earthenware basin, and ladle it from the crater into crystal goblets.

Next, Papa started on Binyamin. "Your geometry tutor says you're absent even when you're present."

"Are you flattering me for my talent as a phantom, Papa?" I could picture Binyamin's full lips curling in a faint sneer. He also knew how to bait and snare.

"I'm saying you need to work at your studies so you can make something of yourself. I've already given up any hope of your helping Miriam and Noah run the business."

"Good. I had no intention of counting money for the rest of my life."

I could feel the fragile peace of *Shabbat* crumbling.

"So what is your intention? To become a beggar? A pickpocket? Because I won't continue to support you much longer." Papa's raspy voice had climbed to a higher octave.

"That's fine with me. I want to enroll in the *ludus* at Capua to train as a gladiator."

My brother has always aimed high. The *ludus* at Capua, the oldest in the Empire, is the school Spartacus made famous. Still, Binyamin is an exceptional athlete, fierce in combative sports like boxing, wrestling, and *pankration,* a strenuous combination of both that ends only when one competitor is either unconscious or dead, unless he manages to surrender first.

But Binyamin, indifferent to the slime and stink of his own wounds, would never surrender. Even as a baby, he never cried. Once, when we were hardly more than toddlers, he escaped from Iphigenia and ran into the street. Before she could catch him, a startled mule kicked him in the chest and sent him to the pavement bleeding. Instead of crying, he tried to run after the mule to kick it back. Today, his noble body, muscular neck, and haughty eyes bristle with power. His flattened but still aggressive nose and the threadlike scar that wriggles across his left cheek only confirm his experience as a formidable combatant.

I could picture blotches of anger spreading from Papa's neck to his hairline.

"A gladiator? Are you crazy? How do you expect to get to Capua? First you'd have to book passage on a grain ship to Rome, apply for an exit visa, and pay the port official in Alexandria for that visa. You'd have to pack your own provisions, cutlery, crockery, a makeshift bed and tent, even your own piss pot. You'd have to wait around on a rat-infested pier, maybe for weeks, until the ship was ready to sail. Then you'd have to amuse yourself on deck for at least a couple of months—that's if there're no storms, G-d forbid, and the sailors have clear skies."

Papa paused for effect.

"On second thought, you could easily amuse yourself onboard. You'd pass the days scheming with every swindler and shooting dice with every trickster, and you'd pass the nights discharging your passion with every whore." Papa forced a laugh, but it sounded false, more like a bray. When he continued, he spoke slowly. His voice was shaking, but his body was motionless.

"And that's just to get to Rome. After that, you'd have to make your way overland to Capua, walking or riding on a hired mule from filthy inn to filthy inn along the entire length of the *Via Appia*. For this, you'd need even more gear: heavy shoes, a broad-brimmed hat, a woolen or leather *paenula* fitted with a hood to protect you from the rain, and a *birrus brittanicus*, a long woolen cloak also with a hood, to protect you from the cold. How do you expect to pay for all that?"

Didn't Papa understand that the logistics were our least concern? But, then again, he was just warming up.

"Don't you realize, Binyamin, I've given you the best of everything, in this, the most splendid city in the world? That you're on a path to ruin? That once you sign a contract and take the oath, you relinquish everything: your citizenship, your freedom, the ownership of your very life? You'll be branded like the lowliest animal and subject to every humiliation. You'll long for the days when your body belonged only to you. And you'll be corralled to breathe the stench and share the lice of the Empire's most wretched criminals, slaves, and prisoners of war."

I hugged my ribs to quell the frisson pulsing through me.

"No, Papa, you're wrong." Binyamin hammered out his words in a cold, brittle staccato, but then his voice took on a zealous tone. "There are more free gladiators than ever in Alexandria, and that's because gladiators are heroes, showered in every city of the empire with fame, fortune, and the company of eager women."

Binyamin might have been thinking of Sergius, the gladiator who'd taken refuge here in Alexandria with Eppia, the senator's wife, who'd given up everything to be with him. But while the love for a gladiator can cut across all social boundaries, most people still regard them, even those most admired in the arena, as outcasts.

"Binyamin, you've reached a new low. You're nothing but a reprobate, a disgrace to your mother's memory, and a stain on our family's name."

I imagined the three of them: my father, his nostrils flared, his lips compressed into a thin line; my brother, his scar blanched against an empurpled face, his eyes glazed and narrowed to hostile slits; and Noah, embarrassed and alarmed, the fine hairs of his polished brow clinging to glossy beads of perspiration. Then I heard two claps in rapid succession, each followed by the clatter of shattering pottery and the tinkle of showering smithereens. That racket could mean only one thing, that my brother had hurled his leather sandals at my father's collection of antique Etruscan vases.

Chapter 3

Friday (*Shabbat*) Evening

I WELCOMED AMRAM at the carved oak entry doors of our limestone townhouse, his yellow face more cadaverous than usual, his stoop more pronounced. Ushering him into the atrium, I seated him on a teak bench among the planters beside the pool. Serving him a silver goblet of pomegranate wine mixed with honey, I hoped to drive away any despondent memories seeing Philo might have aroused and refresh him from having walked from the Great Synagogue in the *Bruchium* Quarter (the Palace Area) to our house in the Jewish Quarter.

Although we have many synagogues throughout the city, none surpass the size and splendor of the Great Synagogue. This double-colonnaded basilica, modeled after the Jerusalem Temple, boasts seventy-one thrones of gold to correspond to the seventy-one elders of the Great Sanhedrin, and a sanctuary so vast that on the High Holy Days the sexton has to wave a flag to signal the thousands of us when to say Amen. My neck cramps just watching him as he stands on the wooden platform above the rest of us who are pressed together in our finery. And my eyes squint as I face east gazing at the dazzling gold and silver threads on the richly embroidered red curtain that covers the Ark. Dulled by the heat, the drone of the sermons, and the rustle of skirts, I feel my head throb and my stomach lurch when the scent of sweat on metallic jewelry clashes with the sweet-smelling pomades, the exotic perfumes, and the fetid breath of dowagers chattering through their rotting teeth.

Still the Synagogue is more than a house of prayer. It's the very center of our community life, the seat of educational and cultural programs and our religious court, the place where Jews come for advice about settling here, and where the members of our various craft associations come to socialize and discuss their business concerns along the airy colonnades of its central hall.

Aside from the Jewish Quarter, which is an exclusively Jewish neighborhood, a substantial number of Jews live to our west in the *Bruchium* Quarter among the city's Greeks. Studded with palaces and gardens as well as the city's grandest institutions and public buildings, the *Bruchium* Quarter embraces the Great Harbor, a circular bay about a mile and a half across. This larger and more eastern of our two harbors is both a public harbor and the port for Roman warships, with an inner harbor for the royal yachts.

In the early morning, when we were kids, Binyamin and I would rush a mule cart and climb over its tailgate to hitch a ride toward the Great Harbor. Binyamin would go first, vaulting into the cart with a somersault, but I'd occasionally lose my perch and tumble onto my buttocks in the middle of the fiery pavement, sometimes on a pillow of spilled grain but just as often on a pile of fresh horse dung. Binyamin would toss handfuls of fodder at me from the scuttle the driver keeps for his mule and further embarrass me with his guffaws until the tide of clip-clopping traffic and the parade of peddlers hauling their handcarts eclipsed him.

Once we'd reach the harbor, I'd admire the curving shoreline, inhale the breath of the sea, and lick its brine off my lips. I'd listen to the ships groan and creak in synchrony with the tide and time my breathing to coincide with its rhythm. I'd follow the gulls, some gliding on the wind high above their shadow, others riding the iron-colored swells or swooping below the surface to return with a silvery fish. And I'd watch the wind darken the water and kick up whitecaps.

Binyamin would watch the warships split the sea as they glided into the harbor. Smaller, lighter, and swifter than the sluggish hulks the Ptolemies built and the clumsy war galleys Mark Antony commanded, these biremes, each with its two levels of oars on each side, its large square sail, and its pointed prow, maneuvered with an agility that would fascinate Binyamin for hours.

The smaller and more western of the two harbors, the *Eunostos* (meaning The Port of Good Return), is our major port for the exchange of goods with the cities of the Mediterranean, the interior of Africa, and the Orient. Like the Great Harbor, it also has an inner harbor, a small, square artificial port called the *Kibotos* (meaning the Box). A canal across the western section of the city connects the *Kibotos* to Lake Mareotis, a huge tidal pool to our immediate south that was formed and is maintained by the gentle flooding of the Nile. During the summer, Amram would take Noah, Binyamin, and me for a daytrip beginning on a ship leaving the *Kibotos* and passing through the canal to serve the string of ports along the lake's marshy banks. I'd watch the sky slide by, listen to the water slap the sides of the ship, and feel the breeze ruffle my hem, tickle the back of my neck, and tangle my hair, all the while imagining miniature villages of fish living in stone palaces beneath the shallows.

When we'd get off at a port, we'd explore the town and then sail back on a different ship, but not before Amram had a chance to taste the local wine mulled with sugar and cinnamon. We'd share a basket of fresh apricots, goat cheese, and olives; and we'd watch the glassmakers, brewers, linen weavers, or papyrus-makers in one of the waterfront factories.

I remember seeing the papyrus-makers: the dusty, walnut-faced workers jabbering away in their gravelly voices, their hands a blur as their needles split the plant stems into strips, the longer and thinner the better. Others busily wove the strips into crisscross-patterned sheets on boards kept damp with muddy water from the Nile. Next, they trimmed the edges of the sheets, pressed out the water, dried them in the sun, and pasted them together side by side with a vinegar-smelling mixture. The last workers then wound the whole length, about fifteen to twenty feet, on a freshly-cut wooden dowel to make a roll about six inches in diameter that any student, scholar, scribe, broker, or merchant in the city could buy. The spicy scent of the freshly-cut wood and the moldy smell of the old sawdust clung to my clothes and filled my nostrils long into that afternoon.

Amram explained to us how these modest factories—scores of them speckle the lake's shoreline—maintain our position as the literary center of the world. No wonder. The sheets and rolls are so perfectly uniform that anyone would be proud to own them. But Noah was impressed by the sheets made from the center of the stem.

"When I grow up," he boasted, "that's the only kind of papyrus I'll buy. I won't write on anything but the smoothest sheets."

If we'd gotten an early start, we'd ride a mule-drawn wagon into the countryside to get a glimpse of the lavish estates, many of them owned by retired legionnaires. I'd pretend to be an explorer commissioned to recover the artifacts of a lost civilization while Binyamin would pretend to be a legionnaire, no doubt a senior centurion commanding his cohort in battle. As a Roman citizen, he'd have been eligible for the legion, but the term of service is twenty five years, too long a commitment for a boy to consider. So he decided to become a gladiator instead.

Lost in the memories of my childhood while Amram sipped his wine, I refocused on him when he put his goblet down on the bench and struggled to unwrap his himation. Underneath it he wore a rumpled tunic of bleached linen decorated with a double blue stripe darned into the material and running down its center front and back. Like most men, he wore it knee-length, fastened at the shoulder with a fibula. He'd girded his at the waist with a heavy leather belt that bunched the extra fabric around his fleshless frame.

"A peaceful *Shabbat*, Miriam," he said after a deep sigh and a long blink over his filmy gray eyes. He's been punctuating his sentences like that since the Pogrom, since its sadness pinched his lips, engraved his forehead, and hung his skin in loose folds along the sides of his mouth.

Despite his greeting, I had to look away when I saw his wizened hands, each finger hardly more than a string of bones. Before taking hold of his goblet again, poor Amram tried repeatedly to brush away the trail of wine stains he'd dribbled onto his tunic. My pity and impatience colliding, I only wanted to still his hands.

To cover my irritation, I asked, "How was Philo?"

His countenance enlivened as soon as he heard my question.

"He's getting old like the rest of us, Miriam. He's almost seventy by now, but he still holds himself upright, and he still participates in every aspect of city life. People see the cuff of his silver beard, the arch of his drooping mustache, and the zeal in his ascetic eyes everywhere. He's at the Great Synagogue, the festivals and banquets, the theater and the games, and, of course, the chariot races, which are his favorite."

I could hardly believe I was listening to Amram. His voice was robust now, full of pride, as if Philo were his father. When he expanded his chest and raised his chin, I could see that a clear moisture had washed away the film in his eyes.

He paused for a moment and closed his eyes. When he opened them and started to speak again, his shift in position told me he'd recalled something about Philo and chariot racing.

"Remember when Philo wrote that column excoriating the reckless fans who, in their excitement, smashed the barriers and charged onto the track? Not only were so many trampled to death, but they triggered a riot."

Amram was referring to the recent carnage in the hippodrome. That's the stadium outside and just east of our city walls. It had once been a mere field, groomed for racing and surrounded by a raised bank for spectators. But the Romans elaborated the site. They built around the elongated oval track an immense stone structure with graduated tiers for seating a hundred thousand spectators. Then they added awnings to shade the wealthy and a protective barrier between the spectators and the professional racing teams that now dominate the sport.

Before the Roman occupation, chariot racing was, like all sports in the Greek tradition, strictly for the pleasure of competing. Papa tells of our paternal great-grandfather,

Binyamin ben Jacob, who was an Olympic champion not only in chariot racing but four years later in the grueling pentathlon. Perhaps Binyamin inherited his athletic prowess from his namesake. But today the races, like all the games, are rowdy spectacles.

Still, I've gone many times. We have twelve or more races in the hippodrome almost once a week, namely on every holiday, festival, and special occasion. General admission is free to the poor so everyone, man or woman, slave or freedman, can bring or rent a pillow and sit in the stands. You can also buy a program with a list of the horses (each with its name, breed, and pedigree) and drivers, their records, and the betting odds for each team. A *centenarius*, a horse that's won at least a hundred races, could be more famous than its driver. Excitement builds as you anticipate the fanfare to signal the first race. You watch the starting gates spring open; feel the ground thunder as the chariots rumble into the arena; thrill in the scent of the richly-oiled leather on the teams' straps, protective gear, and fastenings; and choke on their swirls of dust as the fans' voices merge into a universal roar.

The fans love to see a driver demonstrate his skill by fouling another, even though it's against the rules. Once I saw a driver reach out and grab the bridle of his rival's horse, pull on the bit, and force the rival's chariot back while his own sprang forward. Another time I saw a driver scrape his opponent's chariot with his own, and then, as he surged ahead, he broke the leg of his opponent's horse with one of his wheels. All the while, the fans are playing charioteer themselves, streaming with sweat as they lash their imaginary horses to drive them to victory.

The races are exciting, but the excitement soars when a charioteer, splendid from helmet to boots in his faction's color, captures the inside track, or alas, when there's a spill or a crash. The last time I was at the races, drivers from both the White and Blue factions forced a Red charioteer into the median just as he was about to execute his last deadly turn around the *meta*, the gilded column that's the turning point for each lap. Following the crash, his four-horse team dragged him around the circus while the hooves of the other horses trampled him. Because

Roman charioteers wrap the reins around their waist, he couldn't have freed himself by letting go but would have had to cut the reins with his *falx*, the curved knife every charioteer carries for that purpose. But before he could do that, I heard his chariot splinter, his bones snap, his team of horses stampede, and the spectators yell until their voices croaked. And all I saw were the backs of the fans who, enthralled by the spectacle, stood on their seats flourishing their fists.

Eventually the fans calmed down. A troupe of musicians materialized to entertain us while various crews of slaves drew awnings over the seats for the wealthy, reined in the fallen driver's horses, cleared away his crushed remains and the debris from his wrecked chariot, and raked the track to level its surface and cover the blood-soaked sand and oysters of flesh. Nothing can stop the flies and rats, but to mask the acrid stench of the flesh, blood, and ordure baking under the relentless sun, another crew began to heat on braziers the aromatic cones of the stone pine trees planted for that purpose around the hippodrome.

I had to grab my ankles and drop my head between my knees to keep from getting sick, but many of the spectators took advantage of the break to step around me and swarm to the snack bars beneath the stands. Others waited for a roving food vendor to carve his way through the crowd to peddle pouches of roasted lima beans, the bookmaker in his wake collecting the purses for the next race or consulting his tablet to pay off the winning wagers from the previous race.

The rivalries are keen among the financial backers and betting fans whose loyalty to their favorite faction, Red, White, Blue, or Green, is rooted in their family or craft. Any of them might throw a nail-studded lead missile at a rival faction's team to distract the charioteer or, worse yet, to cause him to spill. But among the charioteers, the rivalries are even more violent. Initially slaves, they can become celebrities and buy their freedom with a sufficient number of victories, each dependent, of course, on surviving their opponents' attempts to force them out of a preferred position. Binyamin says the spills and crashes are so spectacular that no charioteer or team of horses ever dies of old age.

Amram took a last sip from his goblet and handed it to me before continuing his praise of Philo.

"And he can still captivate an audience. He spoke to us about the moral development of man, that once the soul is confined in a body, its purity is threatened by corporeal desires—"

"—*Abba, Abba*, we'd started to worry about you."

Noah must have heard his father's voice from the library. He stumbled into the atrium, his bearing even less certain than usual.

Together, Noah and Amram reminded me of a before-and-after picture. Both are lanky, their arms enclosing their bodies like a pair of parentheses, each face split by a narrow, hatchet-blade nose, the halves reunited by a span of long, overlapping front teeth and a receding chin that makes you believe everything they say. But Noah is clean shaven, his sparse tawny hair as straight and stubborn as the bristles on a paint brush, whereas Amram's hair is the color of mother-of-pearl, its untidy wisps extending from his pink scalp to his lacy Hebraic beard, which he twines when he's deep in thought.

Leaning toward his father, grabbing the bench with one hand, Noah pressed the palm of his other hand to his heart and, in a spray of crumbs, said, "It's late, *Abba*. Come, let's have dinner."

And I wondered why he'd had so much to drink.

Chapter 4

Friday (*Shabbat*) Night

AS NOAH AND I escorted Amram into the dining room, I saw that Phoebe had already served the first course, chilled cucumber slices in a tangy dill dressing, and was bringing in a freshly mixed crater of wine.

Phoebe was the Greek foundling my mother rescued. The long-established practice of the Greeks abandoning their infant daughters had resurfaced in Egypt as a symptom of their hardship under the Roman occupation. Finding her wrapped in a soiled blanket in the *Bruchium* Quarter when she was hardly more than a day old, my mother brought her home and hired a wet nurse for her first three years. Then she herself undertook to rear Phoebe as a domestic slave to assist Iphigenia, who was already getting old.

After my mother's death and until her own nine years ago, Iphigenia minded Phoebe in her own gentle but stern way, along with helping Aunt Hannah manage Binyamin and me. I can still remember Iphigenia as a second mother, a plain woman with the full breasts of a fertility goddess, unobtrusive but never still, her hair streaked with gray, her skin smelling of soap, her cheeks covered with down, her chin sprouting a few errant whiskers, and her spotted hands gnarled with arthritis. Later, when I was five and my father had engaged a tutor for me, he invited Phoebe, at that time ten, to join me in my lessons. Phoebe has given me the confidential ear of a best friend ever since, and when her dimpled smile flashes across her face and crinkles the spray of freckles across her nose, I realize I can view life through a simpler lens.

Papa and Binyamin, by now composed, had taken their places lying side by side on the middle couch. Aunt Hannah held a place for me on the first, and Amram and Noah were to recline on the third, Amram adjacent to Papa. Before taking my place next to Aunt Hannah, I had to review the menu and help Phoebe serve the next course: roast duck stuffed with figs and chestnuts, glazed with a cherry sauce, and accompanied by asparagus in a mustard vinaigrette. After that, we would serve grilled lamb with rice balls rolled in mint extract while the cinnamon tea and sesame cakes topped with currants and dates were being kept warm for dessert.

While Phoebe and I placed the platters on the ivory table and she carved the roast duck, I overheard snippets of the day's news punctuated by bites, sips, and swallows.

"Our business is doing well, Isaac. Noah has been investing our capital at ten percent in mortgages near the agora. The three he closed on this week were for an inn, a glass factory, and just today, the expansion of a Roman-style luncheonette into a larger cookshop."

Good old Noah. True, he invests our capital in the agora for a handsome return, but to first-time borrowers in the outlying neighborhoods, he issues short-term, interest-free loans. That's not all. He offers to pay the tax each year to manumit up to ten of his family's slaves. But few want to leave a household where their needs are met, where they have the ease to rest and study on *Shabbat*, the freedom to earn their own money, the certainty of keeping their family together, the promise of support in their old age, and the gratitude of the people they serve.

I remember when I was a little girl about six years old, and, ignoring Aunt Hannah's warnings to stop playing near the rose bushes, I was attacked by a swarm of bees. Noah visited me every day of my convalescence, bearing a fresh bouquet of carnations and reading to me from *Aesop's Fables*. That's when I began to like the idea of marrying him, when I thought marriage meant always having a playmate, someone to stay with you, tell your secrets to, and share your toys with.

I began to have fantasies then about how we'd play together after we were married: how we'd go to the agora and sample the pastries in every *kapeleion* and the fragrances in every perfumery, how he'd hold my hand and whisper secrets to me when we'd walk in front of our fathers to the Great Synagogue on *Shabbat* and our holy days, and how he'd take me to the harbor in a golden litter and read to me from *The Odyssey* while I watched the gulls frolic beyond the breakers. Still I had trouble imagining him as a hero like Odysseus stringing his bow and shooting it through a dozen axe heads to regain his Penelope.

But when I was twelve, I stopped amusing myself with those fantasies. Noah and I had been walking to the Great Synagogue on the first day of *Sukkot*, Binyamin way ahead of us, Papa and Amram somewhere behind. Amram had tripped and was resting with Papa just inside the Jewish Quarter. When Noah realized we were beyond our parents' supervision, he leaned toward me and whispered that he was going to kiss me. Eager for my first romantic experience, I followed him around a monument and into the inky shadow of a portico. He told me to open my mouth and close my eyes, but instead of kissing me, he stuck his tongue deep inside my mouth and made me gag. When I asked him why he did that, he said he was practicing for when we got married. That's when he started calling me Mimi, as if we'd been bound together by that intimacy, but after that, I didn't even want to hold his hand anymore. So whenever he calls me Mimi, I bristle.

"My Mimi's hair is radiating sparkles of gold tonight—"

Silly Noah. I was wearing a gold net around my bun.

"—I wish she'd set the date."

I hoped Papa hadn't heard that.

"I'm afraid, Isaac. Alexandria is as volatile as ever, intellectually tolerant but politically on the verge of violence. Only a strong arm from Rome can protect us from one faction or another making a scapegoat of us. Otherwise, another eruption against Jews could happen anytime."

This time when Amram spoke, his sigh rose to a low moan.

Amram knew the history of the infamous Alexandrian mob,

24

how even before the Pogrom it had had a centuries-long reputation for brutality with far-reaching political consequences. The provocations may have differed, but the mob's zeal has always been the same.

"The many races in Alexandria are united by only a hatred of Rome and a love of money."

That was Papa parroting one of his clichés. Like most Alexandrians, he relishes the impish wit of our comedians and the rebellious verses of our songsters, who are forever mocking the emperor and the imperial government, but then he regurgitates their quips and epigrams as if they were his own.

"Did you hear about Levi's neighbor?" Binyamin was speaking across Papa and Amram to address Noah. "He was struck down in broad daylight. The one day he went to the *Rhakotis* Quarter without his bodyguard, he was robbed, beaten, and left for dead in a blood-soaked alley."

Binyamin was referring to the third residential quarter to our southwest, all that remains of the old fishing village, pirates' nest, and Egyptian outpost that was known as *Rhakotis* (meaning Building Site). Alexander the Great recognized this two-mile-wide tongue of limestone between the Mediterranean Sea and Lake Mareotis as having the potential to become his great city. But he never had the chance to realize his dream. Before his thirty-third birthday, he succumbed to a fever during a stay in Babylon.

Ultimately, one of his bodyguards, a trusted general named Ptolemy, proclaimed himself King Ptolemy I *Soter* (meaning The Savior) and constructed the city that would be unrivaled for its splendor. But the heaviest burden would fall on the laborers and peasants in the *Rhakotis* Quarter who, in addition to having to pay a draconian share of the taxes, were conscripted to repair the canals, pave the roads, and construct the dikes.

Before Noah had a chance to commiserate, Papa intercepted Binyamin's remark. "Whoever he is, he should have known better than to go to the *Rhakotis* Quarter alone, right Amram?" Papa flashed Amram a knowing nod, but Amram was busy chasing cucumber slices around on his plate.

Papa believes that if he had to learn something the hard way, then everybody else should have learned it then too.

"When Amram and I started our mortgage investment business, I went to the *Rhakotis* Quarter to solicit clients. That, by the way, was the first and only time Amram and I ever disagreed."

How anyone could believe that claptrap, given the duration of their friendship, Amram's measured rationality, and Papa's impetuosity and volatility, was beyond my comprehension. They'd been friends since childhood, when, along with their fathers, they would encounter each other regularly at the Great Synagogue and the Great Gymnasium, the complex that's an educational institution for young men and a center of civic life where Alexandrian men go for relaxation, exercise, and sport.

Aunt Hannah once told me that Amram, who's five years older than Papa, was like an older brother to him, that Amram was the academic one, that Papa had hated school, that Amram had tutored Papa, especially in geometry, and that Amram regarded helping Isaac as his holy obligation. Not that Papa would ever admit to any of that.

Anyway, Aunt Hannah says the substance of a story depends upon who's doing the telling, and the meaning of a story depends upon who's doing the listening. As she tells it, Papa and Amram each ended up in the business of investing in mortgages. Papa struggled as Amram's competitor, but as Amram's business grew, he needed a partner and invited Papa to join him. Still, it was my betrothal to Noah that cemented their partnership.

But as for Papa's claim that he and Amram always agreed, I know firsthand how preposterous that is. I can remember as a child awakening to my father's ear-scraping shouts as he'd argue in the middle of the night with Amram over whether to invest in one property or another, Amram always urging caution. So as I listened to Papa, I suspected that he, not Amram, had suggested venturing into the *Rhakotis* Quarter, and that Amram had even advised against it.

Papa threw back a goblet of wine and smacked his lips

before continuing.

"I was dead set against going, but Amram knew that many hardworking Egyptians could profit from expanding their businesses, that all they needed was the capital. So I went.

"As expected, I encountered the most destitute conditions: the dreariest buildings, the dustiest yards, the grimmest alleys, the foulest gutters, the vilest graffiti, the hungriest mosquitoes, the scrawniest cats, the filthiest children, the saddest drunks, and the oldest whores. Trapped inside the quarter's narrow brooding lanes that twist around a hodge-podge of makeshift dwellings, I thought the houses would topple over and bury me in their stinking rubble. Their windows are small, uncovered, and well above eye level, affording only air, a somber light, and the squalor of the street, not just its screeches and clatters but its festering stenches and smoke from the fish roasting in their courtyards.

"I walked past dozens of toothless, potato-faced men, some shambling about, others squatting amid the rubbish on sun-bleached rocks. Drinking posca from earthen cups, they were throwing knucklebones under a canopy of crisscrossing clotheslines draped with tattered garments. But a spasm of fear ripped through me when I saw just ahead a gang of dagger-wielding thugs storm into a basket shop, the very one topping my list of prospects."

Papa picked up his goblet again. A flicker of confusion puckered his features until he remembered he'd already drained it. Staring ahead while lowering the goblet, he resumed his story.

"They tramped into the shop, their boots grating on the stone doorsill as if they numbered a hundred instead of ten. After that I heard a cacophony of gasps and whimpers, followed by the whoosh and grunts of a scuffle, the smack of fists, the thud of boots, the toppling of merchandise, the slashing of flesh, and the severing of bone, all accompanied by screams so shrill they had to have come from the great pit of Tartarus. Even now I can recall the trill of their blades, a sound I mercifully have never heard since. Then a silence gathered as if a toxic gas had settled over the shop, and deltas of blood began to trickle into the gutter, a tributary of my own excrement adding to the stream.

"Fleeing around the corner, ducking into the nearest alley, I fell to my knees on the backs of my now piss-spattered boots and puked all but my entrails against a filth-stained mud-brick wall. Then, slumping into the pool of my own vomit, a bitter cream still oozing from my nose and tears still cutting tracks through my slime-coated chin, I leaned my head against the wall, gulping for air, daring to stand as I choked down my sobs. Finally, drenched in rancid sweat, I dragged in a breath, swallowed what was left of my spittle, and trudged home. Weaving on wobbly legs through the hot breath of the streets, attacked by a squadron of blood-sucking sand flies, half-blinded by fresh surges of tears, stumbling on every cobble, I bumped into every man, beast, and knot of ragtag boys while lizards shrank from the sight of me.

"That was the last time I ever went to the *Rhakotis* Quarter without a bodyguard, even in broad daylight."

Today, the *Rhakotis* Quarter, where most of the Egyptians who work in the shipyards and warehouses and on the quays still live, continues to be blighted by poverty, pestilence, violence, injustice, and despair.

"I feel so bad for Levi's neighbor, Binyamin, and anyone else who has to venture into that abyss. Corpses surface in the canal there every morning. No one seems to care who's beaten or murdered in the streets. Just last week, a woman was raped and a man robbed. They gouged out her eyes and severed her tongue so she couldn't accuse them, and they castrated him to make sure he wouldn't have the nerve to." Noah's face mirrored the wretchedness of the victims.

Noah feels everyone's pain, but he's so judgmental. I can still see him admonishing me with his chin tucked in and the milky crescents beneath his irises rolling skyward. "Binyamin plays too rough," he'd say. "Besides, raucous play doesn't befit my future wife." Imagine if he'd seen Binyamin and me playing shadow. I'd mimic everything Binyamin did, whether he stood on his head, shinnied up a tree, mounted a sphinx, or threw pebbles at a snake.

And he chides me for going to the agora. "When you're my wife," he says in his flinty tone, "our servants will go so you can stay safely at home." I'm tempted to remind him that his mother and sisters were killed while staying safely at home, but I hold my tongue. He's not the only man to insist on his own way.

"And another thing—"

I shuddered but continued to listen to him.

"We'll never control the street crime in Alexandria until we rein in our entertainers. Whether in the theater or the hippodrome, they cater to the idle and feed the addictions of the morally feeble."

"We have laws in Alexandria, Noah. Isn't it a crime to swear oaths in the agora, and isn't the penalty doubled when the crime is committed by a drunk?"

Didn't I tell you Binyamin knows how to bait and snare?

But Noah ignored him, aiming his criticism next at the religious cults for their extravagant festivals, processions, and games. All spectacles, he was saying, all promoting waste, all fostering greed.

My throat began to tighten. Now Noah was sounding like Philo, who harps on Alexandrians for their unrestrained public behavior and lambastes the city for its garish festivals, calling them excuses for overindulgence, wantonness, and drunken carousing. He says they disgrace their gods and "pander to the belly and the organs below it."

But then the direction of my disgust shifted inward. After all, I, not Noah, was the one evading our long-overdue commitment. So I disliked him even more.

I tuned my ear instead to my father, but that wasn't much better. I could see he was goading Amram.

"So, what did Philo have to say?"

Papa, even more than most Jews, enjoys belittling Philo.

"In many ways his usual, an eloquent justification of biblical teachings using the concepts of Greek philosophy to elucidate their hidden meanings." Once again, Amram's voice was fueled with a high-pitched energy.

"By eloquent, I take it he rambled for hours about a single phrase."

"Now, Isaac, you know our sages bring fresh meaning to a text that way. Tonight he warned us against placing too high a value on wealth and the pleasures it can bring."

"Easy for him to say! He was born into his fortune. Remember Amram, wealth can buy many things, but clean hands aren't one of them."

Another of Papa's clichés.

Amram twined a wisp of his beard and then combed it with his fingers.

"Still, Isaac, remember that story about his wife? She must feel the same way he does. When they were at a banquet where the women were bejeweled from head to toe and someone asked her why she wasn't adorned with ornaments like the other women, she answered, 'The virtue of a husband is a sufficient ornament for his wife.'"

"Sorry, Amram. To listen to Philo you'd think Socrates or Aristotle wrote the *Torah*." Papa dismissed Philo with a flip of his spoon-held hand and a spatter of mustard vinaigrette across the floor.

No surprise there. Papa would never change his opinion about anything, let alone to side with Philo. Anyway, I'd heard enough about Philo so I turned again to Noah. He was still moralizing, but now his target was political corruption.

"The rampant bribery and extortion in Alexandria—"

I turned my head toward Aunt Hannah so he wouldn't see my face redden with reproach, but he must have, because in the corner of my eye, I saw his own face harden into a look that gave me the chills.

"Sometimes, Isaac, Noah sounds like a prig." That was Aunt Hannah in an undertone. As I said, she sees a lot.

Papa flinched, but then his shoulders relaxed, his face softened, and he said, "Of course, Hannah," before turning toward Amram to continue his carping.

"With all the legionnaires roaming the streets and scores of their auxiliary units billeted everywhere carousing and eating like locusts in a field of barley, the streets are still not safe."

"Speaking of the streets, Isaac, you should have seen the Way tonight. Throngs of Greeks and Romans, Egyptians and Arabians, Asians and Afrasians, Iberians and Indians—"

Amram was droning again, counting the ethnic groups on his fingers, a fool's task, given the constant influx of immigrants and the steady flow of up-country Egyptians. Drawn to the venality and riches of this city, all are keen on making their own shrewd fortune here.

"—Carthaginians and Babylonians, Syrians and Assyrians, strolling about, the ladies studded with gems, their graceful necks wreathed in silver and gold, the breeze peppered with their foreign tongues, flashing the colors of their silky robes, everyone celebrating the spicy coolness of the evening in the day-like radiance of the Way's oil-fed torches."

Amram was referring to the Canopic Way, the city's longest and most impressive boulevard, running five miles east to west, from the Gate of the Sun to the Gate of the Moon. He would have had to edge along the Way's marble colonnades, past its stone sphinxes and the polished facades of our most imposing buildings. And sidestep the multitude of soldiers, their faces carved in stone, their red-crested helmets an ever-present symbol of the power of Rome. And elude camel caravans, chariots, mule-drawn wagons, groaning oxcarts, and rumbling drays. And dodge the bearers of sedan chairs and curtained liters, their long, torch-cast shadows hardly a speck on the hundred-foot-wide pavement of granite rectangles. I could picture him zigzagging through a drove of pigs or around a crowd of woolen cloaks. All the while as he crossed the grid of side streets, he'd be embraced by a *Shabbat* sky smeared with stars, safe from the thugs and thieves who'd be inheriting the narrow, twisting alleys of the remote neighborhoods.

"Lots of laborers in the textile factories are getting sick. It's like a death sentence to work there. My Mimi thinks the metallic vapors could be making them sick."

"Binyamin, I always wanted to be a musician, to play the cithara professionally like the citharists do today, but your grandparents thought being an entertainer was too degrading, especially for a woman, even if she was blind."

Enough! I was hungrier than I realized. My stomach was gurgling, and the fat was fast congealing on the roast duck. I took my place next to Aunt Hannah anticipating a savory dinner. I started with the cucumbers, but they were warm and limp. Even the duck was dry. Its cherry glaze had turned to paste, and its stringy fibers kept getting caught between my teeth.

I was sucking them out when Noah stumbled across the room toward me, grasping the back of the couches for balance.

"I don't feel well, Mimi."

I sprang to my feet, instinctively recoiling from his rancid breath. Then, to cover my embarrassment, I shooed an imaginary fly as if it had been the one to provoke my start.

Awash in perspiration, his shoulders more stooped than usual, he didn't have to tell me he wasn't feeling well.

"I have a headache. I want to go home."

"Oh, Noah. Can I get you something? A hot compress? Some lavender tea? A dose of hellebore? Would you like to rest?" Why was I talking so fast? "You're more than welcome to stay over. After *Shabbat*, Papa can send you home in his sedan chair." Wasn't it because I really wanted him to leave?

"No, Mimi. It's only a few blocks. I want to go home, to sleep in my own bed. Please don't be annoyed with me. I don't want to put you out. Besides, it's only a headache."

But the tremor in his upper lip told me it was more. I just didn't know what it was. Not then.

"Binyamin would be glad to accompany you, Noah."

He dropped his eyes and waggled his head.

"All right. While you're saying good-bye, I'll fetch your himation and pack you some food to take home."

I found him leaning against the teak bench among the planters in the atrium. I handed him his himation and helped him wrap it around his body, swathing it over his left arm while picking off a few stray threads. Next I handed him a basket of grilled lamb, rice balls, and sesame cakes and escorted him to our porticoed entrance. Bidding him a peaceful *Shabbat* while he lurched down the stone steps, I slapped the doors closed as he disappeared around the corner of our two streets. But I could still smell his foulness clinging to the plants around the pool as I crossed the atrium to return to the dining room.

And I shuddered.

Chapter 5

Late Friday (*Shabbat*) Night

PAPA, AUNT HANNAH, and Binyamin had each retired to their own suite as soon as dessert was over and Amram had left. Still, the moon was well past its zenith by the time Phoebe and I began a hasty cleanup of the dining room, discarding the food scraps and the puddles of wine left in the goblets and arranging the cutlery and crockery for the maids to wash after *Shabbat*. Phoebe and I would look forward to this time each week as an opportunity to discuss the evening and, for that matter, everything else in our lives.

Once the dining room was tidy, we'd continue our talks in my *cubiculum*, often past the predawn glow until one of us was overcome by sleep or the fragrant light of the *Shabbat* morning began spinning gold on the folds of our bedding. Phoebe would spend the night on the pallet beside my sleeping couch rather than in her own *cubiculum* on the second floor, often dozing well into the morning, filling the air with her sweet breath while I'd gather the wisps of my dreams and comb them for meaning.

Townhouses like ours have their kitchen, public rooms, and the family's private suites on the first floor, the domestic servants' quarters on the second, and an Egyptian-style roof garden on the third. The only difference between ours and others is that we have an exterior rather than an interior courtyard. Papa wanted an unfettered Etesian wind sweeping the scent of roses into our house. Also on the second floor are the guest rooms and the loggia. Overlooking the courtyard and facing north to capture the ocean breeze, the loggia is a favorite spot for Phoebe and me on a summer evening. On a summer morning, our favorite spot is under the roof garden's linen canopy before a breakfast of dates, goat cheese, and muffins flavored with coriander seeds.

Aside from our Phoebe, we have two maids, a cook, a barber for Papa and Binyamin, and a valet and two secretaries for Papa. Like most businessmen, Papa also has two bearers and a sedan chair. Used for transporting himself in style around the city, his is a leather-cushioned chair supported between two carved, polished mahogany poles. His two bearers, along with our gardener and the bodyguard Papa keeps for any of us going out at night or carrying valuables, lodge in the outbuilding where the bearers keep his chair waxed and buffed. But Phoebe is the constant among our staff, my trusted assistant in managing the household.

The only light was the metallic moonlight trickling through the cypress trees outside my sitting room windows and seeping into my *cubiculum*, dappling Phoebe's profile and the mural on the far wall of Homer's Sirens on the rocky coast of their island. This particular morning, she'd climbed onto my sleeping couch so we could lie side by side, embraced by the shadows, gazing at the marble ceiling, watching its tiles change shape.

"Do you ever think about being free, Phoebe? Of Papa's paying the tax for your manumission and setting you up in a business in the agora, like a perfumery? We have the connections for you to import aromatic gums from Somalia, Arabia, and India, and I could show you how to distill them so you could blend and market an exclusive scent."

As I listened to myself, I realized that we'd had this conversation many times before, that I was the one who wanted to be free.

"Why would I want to do that?" She'd drawn her eyebrows together and narrowed her eyes in a slight squint. "To leave the family? You are my family. Your mother saved my life, your father gave me an education, and you're a sister to me. My joy is here, taking care of you like Iphigenia did and being a part of this family and its traditions."

"But you could have your own life, Phoebe."

"I like this life."

"But didn't you ever want to get married? You could if you were free, and then the children you'd have would also be free."

"Well, several years ago I had a crush on a public slave named Bion, a craftsman who repaired scrolls for the Great Library. I met him when I brought our own scrolls to his workshop. As a sideline, he'd repair ones that were privately owned to earn the money to buy his freedom. True, he wasn't the kind of man you'd be likely to notice, but if you did, you'd see that he was handsome in a cherubic sort of way, with rosebud lips and an easy smile that would turn his gold-flecked eyes into fringed slits and his chubby cheeks into pomegranates.

"I'd meet him afternoons under a portico in the central plaza of the agora. We'd share a platter of fruit and pastries at a *kapeleion*, walk along the Great Harbor past the warehouses, cross the *Heptastadion* sometimes all the way to Pharos Island, and then take a litter back. Behind the curtains, he'd pour his heart out to me in a voice trembling with passion. Then he'd cover me with gentle kisses and hold my hand as if he'd never let it go."

"Phoebe, you never told me this! So, what happened?"

"Before he could save the money to buy his freedom, the director sold him to a Jewish craftsman, a sandal-maker from Caesarea, who needed someone both literate and skilled with his hands. Despite our tearful parting, I assured him that he'd be treated well. 'Jews treat their servants with kindness,' I told him. 'Their ethical precepts are grounded in the spiritual elements of their religion. They too are a gentle people repulsed by the harshness of Roman slavery.' And most of all, I assured him that regardless of the price the artisan had to pay for him, which would have been high, he'd still have the opportunity to repair scrolls and earn the money to buy his freedom.

"At first he sent me letters. In his last one, he told me he was saving to buy my freedom as well, but when I told him I'd never leave this household, his letters stopped. That was the last time I heard from him, and that was already a few years ago."

"Do you want to go to Caesarea to see him?"

Phoebe paused to chew on her lower lip. "What is it that you want, Miriam?"

"Well, I know what I don't want, and that's to marry Noah. But it's not just Noah. It's true that I'm not in love with him, but I do trust him and feel connected to him and his father."

"What it is then? He's a good man, and he loves you more than his own life."

I found myself nodding.

"Remember Hector, our tutor?" I asked.

Mirth twinkled in Phoebe's eyes at the mention of Hector's name.

Who could forget Hector, our lovable gorilla, his black hair sprouting everywhere, peeking above his tunic; climbing up his neck, chin, and cheeks all the way to his eyes; spilling out of his nostrils and ears; tumbling down his arms; spreading across the backs of his hands; and cascading down each finger. When Phoebe would botch a recitation of Homer, which she often did, the veins on his forehead would stand out like the tributaries of the Nile. He would stab the air with his cane while the iris of his right eye would spin in an orbit of its own, and she would collapse in a fit of contagious giggles. But Hector did more than make us laugh. He knew everything, not just the language and literature of Homer, but everything else, from Aristotle's natural philosophy to Theophrastus's treatise *On Sense Perception*. Hector described it all, every detail in a patient baritone that could make even a stone cry.

But my favorite subject was anatomy. Hector would tell us about Herophilos of Chalcedon, one of the founders of our great medical school. Herophilos spent most of his life in Alexandria, one of the few cities that permitted the dissection of human cadavers. Because of the tradition of Egyptian mummification, which entails eviscerating the body, the practice was acceptable here until the Romans banned it.

The early Ptolomies would send Herophilos the corpses of their criminals. As if that didn't horrify people enough, some accused him of performing hundreds of vivisections as well. Phoebe's face would pucker when Hector explained what

Herophilos learned about the brain and heart, the arteries and veins, and the eyes and intestines, but I was fascinated by his notion that the soul resides in a ventricle of the brain.

That's when I first became interested in alchemy, although I didn't have a name for it then. Once I learned that the soul resides in the body, I knew that the soul of a metal must reside somewhere in its body too, for didn't Aristotle tell us that all things are composed of the same vital substance? I realized that as long as an imperfect human body can be perfected by the addition of some extract of this vital substance, then an imperfect metal body can be perfected the same way. So instead of studying the healing of humans, I could experiment like Herophilos to study the healing of metals. Then I'd know how to perfect them into silver or gold. That's when I made up my mind that, more than being a wife, I wanted to be an alchemist.

But there was another layer as well, one that would be easier to explain to Phoebe. I didn't want to be a mother and die like mine did.

"Well, Phoebe, Hector told me about mayflies. There are millions upon millions of them living in the Nile, these graceful insects that fold their large, delicately-veined wings together behind their back when they rest. But the adults live only a day or two, not long enough even to eat. They simply reproduce and die. Mayflies remind me of my mother, Phoebe. She was a mayfly. I don't want to be a mayfly too."

"Miriam, your mother wasn't a mayfly. Like Isis (meaning She of the Throne), she was a tender and compassionate wife and mother."

Phoebe loves Isis because of her own history as an abandoned infant. Still, Isis, the Egyptian goddess of motherhood and the patroness of family life, is a favorite among all women here. They identify with her mourning the loss of a husband, protecting the lives of children, and championing the rights of women. Because of Isis, the queens of Egypt had more power and honor than the kings, and the marriage contracts of ordinary women require their husbands to obey them.

Everyone in Alexandria participates in the festivals to

honor Isis. The Fall Festival, the Festival of Seeking and
Finding, is a reenactment of her search for the strewn body parts
of her murdered and dismembered brother and husband, Osiris.
Egyptians believe her tears over his death account for the annual
flooding of the Nile. During the festival, she is said to use her
magic powers to resurrect him.

Isis is also a seafaring divinity. Her Spring Festival, the
Launching of Isis's Ship, is a celebration of renewed life and
marks the advent of our sailing season. In a ceremony for all
Alexandrians, her chief priest names and consecrates a splendid
ship that has been decorated with lights and embroidered sails
and piled high with baskets of spices and other sweet offerings.
After the purification rite, the ship is launched amid libations on
the waves and cheers for a safe sailing season.

Phoebe and I would go to the Isis festivals together.
Afterward, we'd crowd into The Flamingo's Tongue, the
smoke-filled restaurant just east of the *Heptastadion* that seasons
the neighborhood with the aroma of fried onions. There we'd
dine with a view of the lighthouse and the thousands of ships
moored in the Great Harbor, their bumboats swaying in
synchrony with the lapping tide, their rubbery shadows
quivering on the crinkled skin of the water. We'd enjoy the
luxury of a latrine on the premises and a private dining room
crammed with plump couches. A host of jostling waiters would
bear platters of grilled fish, smoked meats, and fried fowl, lithely
shouldering their silvery trays above the clatter of dishes, the
chink of goblets, and the shouts of swilling celebrants.

We'd order dishes like pickled cauliflower and lentil soup
with buttered caraway muffins. The spicy flavors would burst on
our tongues before melding into a savory mixture, rolling down
our throats, and flowering in our chests. Still, we'd save room for
their signature dish, marinated flamingo tongues in a spicy
pepper sauce, a delicacy impossible to find elsewhere in the city.
And we'd enjoy the jugglers, the performing dogs, and the
acrobats in spangled costumes until the afternoon mellowed into
dusk.

By then the vulgarity of the entertainment would spike for

an audience now held aloft by food and wine. The citharists would chant their potpourri of lewd songs, accompanied by the zestful guffaws of revelers, and the mimes would perform their sketches about prostitutes and pimps or adulterous wives and truant schoolboys for the lustful patrons leaping to their feet like hired dancers.

I was already anticipating our next visit to The Flamingo's Tongue, but Phoebe was still focused on my mother.

"Your mother was a goddess, Miriam."

"Maybe so, Phoebe, but I want to do more with my life. I want to make a lasting contribution so my mother's life will have meant more than just producing another generation of mayflies. Still I'm loath to hurt Papa. The future of our family—to say nothing of Noah's—sits squarely on my shoulders, and Papa asks so little of me, only that I marry the most honorable companion a woman could have and carry on the traditions of our two esteemed families."

Phoebe reached up with a jasmine-scented linen square to catch the tears that had begun to sprout in my eyes.

"Papa has had so little comfort in his life. Yet he has given me everything, Phoebe, everything, even my Roman citizenship. That's why I can't free myself from his expectations. What makes matters worse is that my delay continues to baffle and embarrass Noah and his father."

"Oh no, Miriam. They love you."

"They love me, but I see the distress in their eyes. We should have been married by my sixteenth birthday, and already I'm almost seventeen. That's why Papa's been pressing me. I have only this one week, just seven more days, to check with our astrologer and commit to a wedding date."

"You want the kind of personal freedom you've suggested for me, don't you, Miriam?"

"Aunt Hannah always wanted it. Binyamin wants it too. He at least isn't conflicted about demanding it."

"And if you had that freedom?"

"I'd devote my life to studying the properties of metals with Judah. He's the jeweler who at the age of ten began his training with Saul ben Joseph, the master craftsman in the agora. He worked with Saul for ten years and then bought his shop five years ago. Papa and Amram financed Judah's purchase, and this year, when I began collecting the payments from their mortgagors in the agora, I got to know him. But he does more than craft jewelry, Phoebe. He belongs to a secret league of Jewish artisans who study how to perfect the spirit of base metals."

I could see that Phoebe had no interest in the alchemists that Judah had introduced me to and how they sought to apply Aristotle's theory that everything in nature advances toward perfection deep in the ground over long periods of time. Judah and Saul were developing a recipe to accelerate the natural process for perfecting copper into gold. They sought first to deaden the spirit of the copper by blackening it. Only by killing its essential nature could they transform it by stages into its perfect form. Then, through prolonged, gentle heating with arsenic alloys or mercury, a process called tingeing, they would renew the life of the now blackened mass, the *prote hyle*, by impressing it with the spirit of gold.

I could hear my inner voice warning me that I had already said too much, that the League's very existence had to be kept secret so the Gentiles couldn't steal and sell its recipes or accuse the Jews of cheating their customers or conspiring to devalue the currency. So I was glad when, after a polite pause, Phoebe changed the subject.

"So, what did you think of the meal tonight, Miriam?"

"It was lifeless. I'd looked forward to the crispness of the cucumbers, their flavor layered with the dill, and their coolness against the roof of my mouth. Instead they felt spongy. Or was it just me?"

"No, the ingredients were stale; the herbs, dried; and the wine, local. Your father had told me to go to Apollon's *pantopoleion* of all places, instead of to our usual vendors, except for the meat, of course, which I always get from Moshe. Even so, I could see that he was wrapping a cheaper cut of lamb for us, something your father had ordered ahead of time. Your father told me that we needed to economize and to start by cutting back on our food orders."

My throat constricted. "He did what? When did he do that?" I hardly recognized my voice, the pitch was so high.

"Last week. Your father also sold his younger secretary, Kastor, the one who reads and writes both Latin and Greek. He sold him to the Roman civil authorities to work as a clerk in the Public Records Office."

"Which one is Kastor?"

"He's the underfed jackal with the clubfoot."

"I can't believe it." My hands turned to ice.

"You would if you'd heard the fuss he made in the servants' quarters when he had to empty out his things and move into a dingy room, 'the size of a *cubiculum*,' he said, 'in a backstreet of the *Bruchium* Quarter.' He was furious."

At dinner Amram had said business was good, that Noah was closing on mortgages all the time. Why would Papa need money? And why wouldn't he discuss the matter with me first? The same dread I felt before *Shabbat* took hold of me again, this time by the throat.

Chapter 6

Late Saturday (*Shabbat*) Afternoon

AUNT HANNAH AND I would often meet in the courtyard on a late *Shabbat* afternoon to share a light lunch and stroll about the city. This afternoon I found her resting on her favorite chaise lounge, fanned by the date palms' glossy fronds and serenaded by the fountain's babble. The sun brushed her features with gold and spread a veil of warmth across her face.

"Good *Shabbat*, Miriam," she said, sensing my presence before I'd even crossed the threshold. "Come join me. Phoebe brought us each a dish of rice cakes and a bowl of yogurt topped with berries and honeyed walnuts."

I stifled a retch with a hard swallow that sent aftershocks through my bowels.

"I'm too upset to eat," I said, facing her as I took a seat on the edge of her chaise lounge. "I keep obsessing about how I'm going to resolve my betrothal to Noah. I'm too much of a coward to face Noah and Amram, let alone to confront Papa.

"They all think I'd be the perfect wife for Noah, but lately waves of revulsion, even contempt, have rushed through me, only to be followed by ripples of guilt and sorrow as memories of our shared childhood bob to the surface. And I know he senses my estrangement."

My aunt just pursed her lips while I soaked up the silence and let the relief of my confession spread through me. She turned her head as if gazing into the future but then turned back to face me.

"Miriam, when did your feelings for Noah change?"

"I don't think they have. He's still dear to me, but I've

43

discovered another way to love, a way that's different from my feelings for Noah. A way that's a mixture of wonder and excitement, of physical desire and respect. A way that's framed by the desire to belong to someone. A way that's more complex than the familiar companionship I feel for Noah.

"But it's more than my feelings for Noah. I don't think I ever wanted to marry, at least not since I understood what marriage meant. I thought I'd managed to evade the hairy beast, but I see now that it's hunted me down and is poised at my throat. Please, Auntie, tell me what to do."

"You know, Miriam, I never married. I'm not saying I never wanted to, but your grandfather thought your father would be the best one to take care of me, and I suppose he was right. Isaac has been my protector since I was a toddler."

The trace of a smile spoke of their lifetime of mutual affection.

"When I was a little girl and had made a friend, your father would interrupt his studies to take me to her house and then call for me no matter what else he had to do. And after some bullies killed his pet, he became more protective than ever.

"Your grandparents had given him a basenji puppy for his tenth birthday. He would spend hours taking care of his new playmate, feeding it, cuddling it, bathing it, and training it first to stand on its hind legs and then to jump high in the air. But one day, a gang of Greek boys who'd been tormenting your father snatched the dog while he was walking it along our street. A week later they returned the dog in pieces so your father could recognize his beloved basenji and see that they'd tortured it.

"That loss bleached the color out of your father's childhood. Nothing, until he met your mother, could restore his spirit, not running on the beach, catching fish on the lake, or riding oxcarts in the countryside, all jaunts he'd shared with his basenji. Your father emerged from the horror with a heightened sense of vulnerability and the dread that harm could come without warning to anyone or anything he loved.

"I saw his obsession intensify when he courted your mother. He became wary, overprotective, even officious. She came from a family that had once owned and operated a fleet of freighters in the eastern Mediterranean. They'd been wealthy but had lost too many ships to storms in the Aegean and piracy along the Anatolian coast to meet their expenses. At first our parents objected to the match. They thought her family's losses presaged a future of bad luck. Besides, your mother, even as the only surviving child, had a meager dowry: some Alexandrian pearls, clothing, and cash, but no landed properties. Nevertheless, they acquiesced. She was after all a Jewess, a member of our tribe, and a Roman citizen, and your father was smitten with her. But years later, with her two stillbirths, your father would wonder whether our parents had been right, that her family had been doomed.

"In the meantime, your father doted on me all the more. When I got a little older, he surprised me with a cithara and shared his music tutor with me. So I can't say I've missed much. Although I didn't have the opportunity to follow my dreams as you do, I was free to study music, a pleasure I could curl myself around, one that's helped suppress my other yearnings. And while exempt from domestic duties, I still had the satisfaction of helping to rear you and Binyamin."

She grasped my hand as if she'd seen it resting in my lap.

"But, Auntie, did you ever want to marry?"

She pushed aside her bowl of yogurt. Inhaling deeply, she closed her eyes and tipped her head back, as if gathering the details of a dream long since anesthetized. When she lowered her chin and opened her eyes, her lips had relaxed into a faint smile, her complexion had turned to a rosy blush, and her eyes sparkled like sequins.

"I once had a suitor, Miriam. You've heard of your great-grandfather, the Olympic champion Binyamin ben Jacob? He had a brother, Pinchas. My suitor was his grandson, Samson. Samson had started a trading company to transport goods by sea between the Mediterranean and China. Instead of using intermediaries to and from the Indus River to move the goods by caravan across Asia, his ships would sail around the tip of the Indian peninsula.

"Isaac and your grandfather Asher were concerned that Samson would be away from Alexandria for long periods of time, that he'd be busy managing the offices he'd have to establish in the commercial centers along his route. Worse yet, they imagined him leaving me in one of those cities, beyond any point where they could watch over me.

"Samson came to visit several times. Some afternoons, when we'd sit across from each other in the courtyard holding hands and sipping tea, he'd speak to me about his future in the fine-textured, resolute voice of a politician. Some evenings, when we'd walk along the harbor, he'd explain his plans in an intimate whisper, his lips close to my ear, his dulcet words carried on the current of verbena that scented the air around him.

"But your father and grandfather didn't trust him. They said his laugh was too loud, his nose too long, his palms too damp, his cologne too strong, his hair too greasy, his manner too familiar, and his tongue too glib. That he seemed more interested in my dowry than my welfare. That he could beget children with foreign women along his trade route and force me to adopt them so they'd be Roman citizens. That our family would be better off investing all of its capital in a business for Isaac rather than dividing it up to give me a dowry. So one day Samson and I were planning a future together, and the next day he was gone."

My poor Auntie, living all these years with an unfulfilled dream. Still, my sadness for her paled alongside the resentment I felt toward my father and grandfather. I was about to ask her whether she'd considered marrying Amram after Leah was killed, but I didn't have the chance because a moment later, she'd shrugged off the memory of Samson and had refocused on my quandary.

"Still, I'm wondering, Miriam. What part about being married distresses you?"

I reached into the corners of my mind for something I could put into words.

"It's the part about being a mother. Perhaps I resent having to be a mother when I didn't have one myself, or perhaps I just don't believe I'd know how to be one. What I feel though is fear. I'm afraid that what happened to my mother will happen to me, that I've inherited her fate. Everyone, even Papa, says I'm just like her. I told Phoebe that I didn't want to be a mayfly, but the truth is I'm afraid I would be a mayfly."

"Just because you look like your mother, Miriam, doesn't mean your life has to turn out like hers. Besides, you don't have to live as she did to honor her memory. She made a life that had meaning to her, and you can make a life that has meaning to you."

Aunt Hannah's pause, deep breath, and shift of position told me she was about to tell another story about my parents.

"When your mother felt life quicken inside her, she went to her astrologer, who told her that she'd have a daughter with great gifts, one whose contributions would be famous for centuries but who would also experience great losses. So she knew your life would be exceptional. To bless the birth, she and your father commissioned the writing of a *Sefer Torah* (meaning Book of the *Torah*) for the Great Synagogue."

I'd heard the story about the *Sefer Torah* many times. That my parents had hired the most pious scribe in Judea to make a copy of the *Torah* (The Five Books of Moses), our holiest text and the foundation of our legal, ethical, and religious codes. Because every mark, including all 304,805 stylized Hebrew letters, is divinely inspired and infused with arcane meanings, the copy must be perfect. And everything, the quills, the parchment, and the strands to sew the panels together, must come from kosher animals.

My parents also arranged for a community celebration upon completion of the *Sefer Torah*. The thousand-year-old tradition of singing, praying, and dancing before the Holy Ark would take place on the first anniversary of the birth. But instead of our parents dedicating the *Sefer Torah* to the birth of Binyamin and me, my father, alas, ended up dedicating it to the memory of our mother and sending Amram in his place to claim the honor of copying the last few letters.

But I'm getting ahead of Aunt Hannah's story.

"Your father bought a well-trained doula to assist Iphigenia. He also hired a midwife reputed to have miraculous powers. He gave your mother charms to protect her from Abyzou, the infertile demon responsible for miscarriages and infant mortality. He arranged for your mother to have the purest foods, and when her time drew near, he bought the freshest herbs to start her labor and ease her pain. But beginning a day or two after your birth, the heat from her heart began to escape, her pulse rate increased, and she began to vomit.

"As your mother's strength ebbed, your father would stumble through the house, carrying her from room to room, sometimes begging, other times commanding her fever to go away. Until then, death had been a misfortune that happened only to others.

"Her suffering ended when she died, but your father's had only begun. Raw grief took hold of him. For weeks thereafter, he would tear at his clothes, and smothering himself in her soiled linen, filling his nostrils with her scent, he'd pound his body with his fists as if to pulverize the grief and expel it through his pores. All the while, he'd be either gasping and heaving in a convulsive wave of sobs or whimpering for the Yocheved who'd abandoned him. He emerged from this acute phase of anguish with a romanticized image of your mother, like the bronze statue in his study, that no one, not you or Yocheved herself, could possibly live up to. That's when his fear of losing a loved one hardened into an obsession.

"I suspect, Miriam, that since your earliest days, you've been carrying the double burden of dealing with his obsession and living up to his myth, to say nothing of your having to suffer the ambivalence he must feel toward you and Binyamin. Although these circumstances have fostered in you a remarkable sensitivity—"

(She meant the way I'm so vulnerable to criticism. As if I were porous, she says.)

"—and a perfectionist's sense of order—"

(She meant the way I arrange my things symmetrically and

count everything, like my steps when I walk around the house.)

"—they have undermined your self-confidence and sense of independence."

(She meant the way I fret so much about my relationship with Papa.)

"So why isn't Binyamin like that too? He wears a crust of confidence and flouts all boundaries."

"Because your mother's death affected him differently. You know Binyamin was a breech baby. That's why his Roman name is Agrippa, meaning 'born feet first.' Consequently, he blames himself for your mother's death. So Binyamin's recklessness could be his way of inviting retribution."

"Oh, Auntie, I wish you could tell Papa that Binyamin needs his forgiveness, not his reprimands, and that the woman of his bronze statue is an invention. But he's armored in pride and fortified by wrath. I pity him, that his solace should derive from a figment of his imagination. But I'm also angry with him, angry that he baits Binyamin and counts on me to fulfill his fantasy. All I know is that I'm sick at heart for being expected to assume the life he's cast for me, and disgusted with myself for being too spineless to defy him."

The way Aunt Hannah pressed her lips together told me that she too had no ready solution.

"Come, Miriam. Let's take a walk along the waterfront so the *Shabbat* breeze can tousle our hair."

Chapter 7

Later Saturday *(Shabbat)* Afternoon

MY MOOD LIFTED as soon as we stepped into the brilliant light of a *Shabbat* afternoon and I heard the heels of our sandals clacking on the rough cobblestones. Aunt Hannah at my side, cupping my left elbow with her right hand, we threaded our way north and west through the Jewish Quarter toward the shoreline of the *Bruchium* Quarter. Of the three residential quarters in Alexandria, ours, also known as the Delta Quarter, is the district Ptolemy I pledged to our people to encourage us to settle here. Most of us, about twenty percent of the city's population (our largest community outside of Palestine), prefer to live in our own quarter, where we are free to observe our customs and obey the laws of our Council of Elders.

We pride ourselves on living in the finest quarter of the city. We're on the coast and farthest from the main necropolis. Alexandrians have been burying their dead there for more than a century, whether in multi-chambered underground tombs of stone decorated with the scenes and symbols of Egyptian funerary art, or in simple, earth-covered pits. In the Jewish Quarter, we can inhale the scent of the sea instead of the stench of the embalming workshops.

"Auntie, we're passing Levi's house now. The ground is a little uneven, so hold onto me with both hands."

"Have their roses grown taller this year?"

I could swear my aunt could see.

"And Miriam, do I hear a raven croaking over there?"

She was pointing to a crooked pine tree a few feet from our path. It was laden with cones, a brown-necked raven concealed in its crotch.

"A plump one, Auntie with a proud stance; long, pointed wings; a thick, sharp beak that sets its face in a frown; and a blunt tail."

After a few more blocks, we passed on our right the barracks and armories of the Roman fleet, which dominate the eastern waterfront of the *Bruchium* Quarter. When we reached the beach, we lingered under the fronds of a date palm, inhaling the briny smell of the damp sand, almost tasting the ropes of kelp stranded on the beach. Listening to the surf lap the shore, we basked in the gentle sea breeze as it ruffled the hems of our himations.

For a moment, I watched a family of bathers, the children's wet hair sticking to their faces like black ribbons as they frolicked on the massive marble steps that descend into the salty water. They reminded me of when Iphigenia would take Binyamin and me to swim there. Until she'd call us, I'd ride the waves like an alighting gull while pretending to be Thessalonike, the legendary mermaid who calms the seas for sailors. But Binyamin would continue swimming even as Iphigenia stood near the edge of the steps flailing her arms to get his attention, even as the wind whipped her tunic, slapped her broad cheeks, and snapped plumes of her gray-streaked hair across her forehead. He'd tunnel under the waves and cut through the foam like a razor until she'd have to send for Papa's bodyguard to fish him out. By then his ginger curls would be stiff with salt and his face bronzed by the sun.

Of course, that's not how Binyamin would tell the story. He'd say that by the time we walked to the beach—Iphigenia wouldn't dare let us rush a mule cart—he'd have barely enough time to get wet before she'd say it was time to go. "We could've found our own way home," he'd say. "So why couldn't she let us stay?"

Anyway, once we got home, Papa would ground him for a week.

"Auntie, the sea is a shimmering lake this *Shabbat* afternoon."

The sun was also stroking the tiny lines of her brow, while the breeze was loosening tendrils of her caramel hair, some veined with silver, others with gold.

"The metallic luster of your hair, Auntie, reminds me of the work I'm doing with Judah."

Interest lifted the corners of her mouth.

"Judah and Saul are studying how to perfect copper into gold. Judah lent me the League's notes from Aristotle's *Meteorologica* that detail how metals are perfected deep in the ground when the right mixture of earths and waters congeals. If that process is interrupted, a rudimentary form of the perfect metal, a base metal like copper, results. He also lent me his own notes on the recipe he and Saul have devised to perfect copper in a bath of mercury. But first, they have to extract the mercury from cinnabar, its brick-red ore. I'm so excited because just before stowing the scrolls and preparing for *Shabbat*, I recorded my own design for an apparatus to roast the cinnabar and collect the mercury vapors safely. So, as soon as *Shabbat* is over, I can begin constructing it."

Aunt Hannah swept a ribbon of hair away from her eyes, but the wind blew it back again.

"Tell me, Miriam, why is alchemy so interesting to you?"

My aunt has always been interested in anything that interests me.

"Alchemy is the search for both material and spiritual perfection. Saul and Judah are interested in perfecting metals. By transferring the appropriate spirit (vapor) to a base metal like copper, they hope to transmute it into gold. I'm interested in perfecting not only the body and spirit of metals but the body and spirit of humans as well. My fascination with the human body began when I studied anatomy with Hector."

"How can learning about the body and spirit of metals help you understand the body and spirit of humans?"

"One principle of alchemy, Auntie, is Aristotle's Unity of Nature, that all things, whether animal, vegetable, mineral, or human, are variant forms of the same vital substance. That's why learning about one can teach you about everything else.

"I want to make it safe to study metals. If I can make an apparatus for experimenting with metals safely, it might prevent the sicknesses that are afflicting our alchemists. And not just the alchemists but the dyers in our textile factories. They too are showing the same deadly symptoms. I think they're being poisoned by the metals in either the dyes or the mordants that set the dyes on the fabrics.

"Only the laborers who work with the dyes are getting sick. Some, like Judah's cousin David, began to drool and retch, then to vomit up a greenish-yellow cream streaked with blood. David's urine also turned dark red until he couldn't urinate at all. He died in a delirium shortly after that, during a convulsion when his heart failed. David's brother-in-law, Uri, also died that way, but before that, he'd lost all feeling in his body except for a burning sensation in his hands and feet. The burning was so severe that, in his delirium, he tried to cut off his feet. Scores of workers are suffering like this."

My aunt wrinkled her prissy nose. Evidently the clinical details were too much for her, especially on *Shabbat*.

After a hard swallow, she said, "So, have I met your Judah?"

"No, Auntie. That's another problem. Papa would never permit him in our home. First, Judah is a bastard. No one, including Judah himself, knows anything about his father."

My aunt's eyebrows rose slightly.

"His mother was Jewish, a silversmith named Ruth who was orphaned when her parents were crushed by an overloaded oxcart. It flipped over right in front of their butcher shop one summer evening as they were accepting a delivery of ice. So, without a dowry, Ruth couldn't marry. Then, more than a decade ago, she herself died of pneumonia. She'd caught a chill that depleted the heat in her body and generated more phlegm than her physicians could purge in time to save her.

"Second, Judah is neither a Roman citizen nor a member of any other privileged class, so he's subject to the *laographia*."

By now, my aunt had started to work the inside of her cheek.

The *laographia*, or poll tax, is one of a complex array of taxes, charges, and surcharges imposed on Roman Egypt, a humiliating tax on all accountable males between the ages of fourteen and sixty, including slaves. The tax collector, selected for his raw brutality and accompanied by soldiers and armed guards (ostensibly for his own protection but serving to terrorize the taxpayer), resorts to any cruelty to exact payment. He knows he has to make up the money he fails to collect but he can keep any surplus for himself.

"Just last week, Auntie, there was yet another spectacle in the agora. The tax collector filled a huge basket with sand and lassoed it around the necks of an entire family, the wife, children, and parents of a fugitive of the *laographia*. Sinking under its weight in the relentless sun of the open marketplace, they suffered a prolonged and humiliating death. People jostled for a space, bobbing and squatting for a glimpse, stretching their own necks like turtles to see what was happening, but no one dared to offer any help beyond a pitying glance, not even a cup of water, for fear of being held liable for the debt or of being tortured for information on the fugitive's whereabouts."

Tax collectors have continued whipping their victims even after death to extort payment from relatives for the release of the body. Aside from having to face one of these spectacles, we all run the risk of encountering an acquaintance in the agora, someone the tax collector has reduced to slavery. Now a beast of burden, he plods through the crowd lugging an unwieldy load on his twisted back.

"So apart from collecting the mortgage payments on Judah's stall, Papa wants me to have nothing to do with him. To Papa, he's just another bastard with no future."

After listening judicially, Aunt Hannah tilted her head back slightly and asked, "So, how do you feel about Judah?"

How could I explain my feelings to her? That until I met Judah, love was an abstraction to me, the substance of myth, legend, and my own embryonic fantasies. But when I met him, a flutter deep inside my belly stirred the rest of me to life and launched a longing both mystical and earthy, passionate and tender, shy and eager.

So I didn't say anything. Instead, for that split second, I was grateful that my aunt was blind, that she couldn't see the blush burning through me, or the image of Judah in my eyes: his thick black curls glossy with sweat, his luminous green eyes framed by a dreamer's lashes, and the precise contours of his body beneath his coarse gray woolen tunic.

Aunt Hannah waited as if listening for another raven.

"Miriam, I hope you're not confusing an interest in alchemy with a lust for Judah."

"Come, Auntie. Let's finish our walk."

Continuing westward along the shore, we reached our favorite stone bench in the gardens along the base of Point Lochias, the promontory of royal land that belonged to the Ptolemies and where the Roman governor now lives. Thrusting its peninsula into the sea, the Point's arc shapes the eastern boundary of the Great Harbor. Here, lining the harbor, the palaces are a dazzle of light, each limestone, granite, and marble exterior radiating the scent of warm stone, each linked to another through a maze of porticoes and colonnades, each casting its slanted silhouette upon its gleaming neighbor.

Also casting their silhouettes are groves of cypress, olive, and pine trees populated by marble statues who look as if they too, like me, can hear the whisper of each fountain's iridescent spray, breathe in the heady fragrance of the roses, and watch the swans glide on the silvered surface of each quiet pool. Like the pools in our quarter and the fountain in our very own courtyard, the source of water for these fountains and pools is the Canopic branch of the Nile. Via a twelve-mile canal and an elaborate labyrinth of tunnels, the Nile finds its way to hundreds of underground stone cisterns in every neighborhood of the city except our most destitute outskirts. There the tenement dwellers must fetch their water from a stagnant canal lacy with scum.

Following the gulls wheeling overhead, calling to one another, spiraling toward the docks, each spreading a ripple of foam as it settled on the water, I took the moment to watch the activity in the harbor. Among the thousands of vessels, a heavy dory with extra-long oars was towing a naval ship to moor her nose-first to a huge stone ring on the marble quay. At the same time, a procession of brown, bare-chested stevedores unloaded a cargo ship. Already moored, her gangplank lowered, she'd been carrying camphor, jade, and silk from China and cotton, cinnamon, spikenard, and pepper from India, treasures destined for the governor's household. And on the poop of a third ship entering the harbor, the grateful captain, his feet planted in the bold stance of a sailor, was performing a post-sail sacrifice.

By the time Aunt Hannah and I got up from our bench, I'd hardly a thought about my own Strait of Messina, about my own Scylla and my own Charybdis.

Chapter 8

Early Sunday Morning

I HAD NO INKLING that Sunday morning that our house had been burglarized and that the theft would lead to an even greater calamity. As I crossed the courtyard in the Sunday morning stillness and entered the library's main level, I was aware of only the hem of my tunic sweeping across the cool mosaic floor and my footsteps resounding against the marble staircase that leads to the upper level, a gallery supported by fluted Doric columns. Looking up toward the white plaster ceiling, I saw three walls of polished acacia cubbies, each crammed with papyrus scrolls, their wooden dowels jutting out, their leather tags entangled. And resting against the gallery's back wall I saw the moveable, shoulder-high platform ladder hooked onto the brass rail that runs along each of the three walls.

A lone moth flickered in the glow of an oil lamp lit before *Shabbat* and left to burn after the evening's three stars had ushered in the new week. The feeble light barely washed the round cherry wood table and surrounding chairs, let alone Aunt Hannah's spindly-legged chair that backs against the north window and the open mahogany hutch atop its matching cabinet along the western wall. The hutch's upper shelves displayed what remained of Papa's collection of Etruscan vases. The lowest shelf was mine. Papa had it divided into several compartments, some for stowing my primers, notes, and souvenirs, including the ceramic figurines that had belonged to my mother. But one cubby was for the bronze pen that had been my mother's, a bottle of carbon black ink, and most important, the scrolls for my work with the League. Despite the oil lamp and the blush of dawn edging the walls, the library smelled of darkness.

I reached into my compartment for the scrolls, the three of them, the two from Judah and the one of my own. So accustomed was I to the coolness of my pen and the familiar contour of the ink bottle impressed against my palm that I didn't immediately notice that the rest of the compartment was empty.

But then I did.

My eyes raked the compartment from side to side, front to back.

The scrolls were gone.

All three of them.

I hardly recognized the sound of my own shriek as waves of disbelief and then alarm spread through my chest like a seismic shock. I pressed the back of my hand against my open mouth, biting the knuckle of my index finger, all but breaking the skin to stifle the howl welling up inside me. Otherwise I'd have stirred not only the entire Jewish Quarter but the early Ptolemies buried in the Old Necropolis just east of our quarter. At the same time, sparks snapped inside my head as the scene before me spun farther and farther away before zooming back on fresh waves of disbelief and alarm.

How could the scrolls have disappeared?

Once more, I felt the inside of the compartment, this time leaning against the cabinet so my flattened palm could reach all the way back to verify the void. My eyes could have deceived me, but never my hands, certainly not twice.

Nothing.

Where could the scrolls be?

In my panic, I had to search somewhere.

I dashed to the staircase and charged up the steps, tripping on the hem of my tunic, gouging my forehead against the edge of a riser, grabbing for the banister, hoisting myself up, and scrambling onto the gallery.

My hands seized scrolls, bunches of them, tugging them free. First, a few tumbled out, then a rush of them, scores, hundreds, even thousands cascading everywhere, over the ladder, some rolling across the floor and bounding down the steps, others flying over the balustrade, thundering against the table, gashing its surface, chipping its rim, bouncing off, splintering the glass lamp, knocking down a chair, first one, then another.

Followed by a burst of them. Like missiles, aiming for the rest of Papa's Etruscan vases, and Holy of Holies, my mother's figurines.

Shattered.

Then the walls spun, the floor canted, the light faded, and darkness swallowed me.

When my eyes opened, I was startled to find Phoebe crowned with debris hovering over me, her consoling presence framed by the floral motifs on the plaster ceiling.

"Miriam, what happened?"

The details hit me like a one-two punch that made me wish I were unconscious again. The first punch was a replay of the morning's events but in reverse: my parents' treasures shattering, the thousands of scrolls spilling over the balustrade, my forehead stinging against the edge of the riser, my dash to the staircase, and my reach into the empty compartment. The second punch flashed images of my routine for storing the scrolls before *Shabbat*: rolling them up, tying each with its silk sash; turning from the table, always from the same chair; walking the three steps to my compartment; bending to check that the inside was clean; and stowing each one, the pen and ink going in last.

I found my tongue, but could utter only a staccato. My breath was still trapped inside my rib cage.

"Scrolls gone."

Could Phoebe hear me over the buzz in my head?

"We can buy new ones."

"No. League's scrolls. Secrets valuable. Black market. Jews in danger."

I dreaded facing Judah. He'd entrusted me with them. I'd promised to return them this afternoon. How could he rely on me again? How could the League? How could anyone?

"Who could have taken them, Phoebe? Who in this house would betray me like this?"

The thought throbbed like a toothache.

Chapter 9

Late Sunday Morning

OTHERS IN THE household were taken aback by the disappearance of the scrolls—there was a lot of tsking and head shaking—but I was stunned as if I'd been beaten into unconsciousness in the darkest alley of the *Rhakotis* Quarter and left there to die. Nevertheless, I'd promised to return the scrolls to Judah that afternoon, an occasion I would otherwise have looked forward to with a starved longing. I had to see him, if only to explain why I wasn't returning them.

I remember asking the maids to take extra care with my grooming that morning, as if my appearance could distract Judah from the missing scrolls. They bathed me, rubbed my face with a pumice stone to remove the stray hairs around my eyebrows and upper lip, and anointed me with Arabian fragrances. While I watched in a polished bronze mirror, one plaited my hair with ribbons to make a braided crown that she fixed in place with beaded pins. The other heated a metal rod and, holding it by its wooden handle, wrapped locks of hair around it to set a row of screw curls across my forehead to cover the gash. Then they dressed me in a sleeveless blue linen *tunica interior* over which I wore a white silk chiton girded under my breast and pooling in soft folds to my ankles. Finally, they arranged a strand of lapis lazuli around my neck, dressed my ears with matching stones, clad my feet in ankle-length pigskin boots, and enveloped me in a light woolen himation fastened at the shoulder with my mother's fibula.

Propelled by a gritty sea breeze that chilled the nape of my neck and flattened my skirt against my calves, I walked south to the Canopic Way, where I turned west toward the *Bruchium* Quarter. Led by my shrinking shadow, I passed the Great Synagogue and neared the campus of the Great Gymnasium, which is south of the palace gardens that Aunt Hannah and I visited the day before and across the Canopic Way from the Park of Pan.

Sometimes, on my way home from the agora after seeing Judah, I would stop at the Park of Pan, the site the early Ptolomies created to honor their goat-like god of shepherds, pastures, and flocks. As I'd climb to its summit along a walkway shadowed by dwarf pines, I'd spiral around its fir-cone shaped hill, passing the grotto dedicated to the playful Pan, and marvel at the series of artificial terraces and waterfalls wreathed in rainbows. All the while the turtledoves in its gardens and the blackbirds along its secluded sylvan pathways would accompany me with their songs. When I'd reached the summit, I'd look out at the magnificent view encircling me, especially at the walls that once enclosed the city's sprawl, and imagine my own future like the city's, pressing to expand beyond today's constraints.

The walls date back more than three hundred and fifty years to the time of Ptolemy I. Standing in triplicate and shouldering towers at frequent intervals, they form a twelve-mile semicircle around the city. (No walls enclose the seaward side.) Three gates pierce the walls: the Gate of the Sun at the eastern end of the Canopic Way, the Gate of the Moon at its western end, and the Mareotic Gate at the southern end of the Street of the Soma. On the eastern and western sides, the walls soar to two stories, but on the southern side, where armed ships guard Lake Mareotis, they level to only one.

But whether or not I'd stop by the park, my palms would dampen whenever I passed the grove of marble columns that fronts the Great Gymnasium. I'd recall the *pankration* competition in its *palaistra*, the Gymnasium's school for combative sports. Binyamin had his very first bout there shortly after entering ephebic training, the Gymnasium's physical and academic preparation for young men of privilege. During the bout, he distinguished himself as an accomplished athlete against another ephebe, Titus, who along with Binyamin had just had his long, childhood hair shorn at their induction ceremony.

At first they seemed well matched, the fair, husky Titus hammering Binyamin's face with a few left jabs, a thread of blood squiggling from Binyamin's eyebrow, Titus driving his fists into Binyamin's midriff, and Binyamin pounding him with some solid body punches. But then Binyamin caught him with a sudden left hook to the jaw, a straight right to the nose that snapped his head back, and a strangle hold that sent him to the mat. Permanently. Binyamin's face froze in numbed disbelief and my father's foam-flecked lips twisted in horror. A mass of oozing wounds was all that remained of Binyamin's schoolmate.

By the time I neared the intersection with our other main thoroughfare, the Street of the Soma, the sun had inched its way up the sky enough to bake the pavement and coat my throat with dust. In front of the Museum (meaning Shrine of the Muses but serving as our academy for scholars) and the adjoining Great Library, I carved my way through a thickening crowd of tourists. Some in robes, others in turbans, they were shouting in a host of languages, perhaps hoping for a glimpse of Hero or one of the free-roaming exotic animals that the scholars keep in their private zoo.

I had to wait at the intersection for a curtained litter to pass. While the *pedisequi*, the slaves who trot ahead of and alongside their master's litter, were parting the crowd with their long bamboo canes, I could gaze across the Way at the Soma, the sacred precinct Ptolemy II built to honor Alexander the Great.

The Soma is the magnificent walled precinct around the mausoleum itself, a funereal temple built of the finest Greek and Egyptian marbles and furnished with the most exquisite mortuary relics. The body of Alexander was interred under the temple in a cool recess at the end of a long, sepulchral anteroom called the Place of Lamentation, a flight of steps down from the temple's colonnaded courtyard. Although it became the resting place as well for the later Ptolemies, the Soma was dedicated to the worship of the divine Alexander.

But today Alexander lies in a looted vault with a broken

nose. With the insolvency of his government, Ptolemy IX *Soter* II or *Lathyros* (meaning Green Pea) seized Alexander's gold coffin, melted it down for coinage, and replaced it with one of crystal. The second insult occurred when Augustus, in his clumsy eagerness to examine Alexander's mummified remains, crushed part of the noble nose. Still, tourists this morning, like every morning, are lining up along the walls around the Soma to pass through its heavy bronze doors. If they're looking for inspiration in the restrained beauty of the temple, its clouds of lavender incense, its floors inlaid with mother-of-pearl, its priests' undulating robes, or the soul of its immortal hero, they'll have to find it as well in the odor of ancient dust, the must of under-ventilation, the crush of sweaty bodies, and the greasy fingerprints on Alexander's coffin.

Just as the litter was rounding the corner, another procession appeared, this one a motley parade of the crippled and the sick, each carrying a gift while casting a deformed shadow across the pavement. As they hobbled northward on the median strip of the Street of the Soma, I noticed among them a dull-eyed, ashen man, hardly more than a crooked skeleton. Wincing as he leaned forward to support his tottering companion, he nevertheless offered him a tentative smile. As if in rehearsal, each for his own death, the troop was heading for the Temple of Isis on Pharos Island and the noon opening of its sanctuary for private prayer and meditation.

While waiting, I found myself absorbed in my favorite fantasy, that of spending my life with Judah, all the while sensing an odd tingle of both pleasure and pain. I imagined him in the dim lamplight loosening my hair, it spilling into his hands and stirring his passion. Drugged by the scent of him, I'd surrender in a flush of longing. Moving above me, his hands everywhere delighting me, guiding me, he'd penetrate my most private chamber, losing himself inside me, spreading his heat through me. Our bodies would rock as one, riding waves of heightening pleasure until that crest of ecstasy when the world would quake and the shudder of fulfillment would pulse through us. Then, against the tousled sheets, in a daze of exhaustion, I'd dissolve into his tenderness, and floating in his warmth and the sweetness of his breath, I'd fall asleep wrapped in his arms.

Most of the time the fantasy would end there, but sometimes I'd extend it to our mornings together, my awakening at his side, our working in his shop, his crafting metals, together our fashioning experimental apparatus. I'd repeated this fantasy so many times, occasionally elaborating it, more often keeping it simple, varying it only as to whether we'd someday transmute the copper into gold.

Continuing with my liquid thoughts, dreaming my way back to earlier that year, I re-lived my first encounter with Judah, that unexpected ache when I walked into his shop. He raised his lids to look at me and then squared his shoulders with a slow, deep, almost guttural intake of breath and an even slower exhale. Later, as I was leaving, he leaned toward me. That sensation of his nearness, close enough for our air to mingle and for his hand to brush against mine when he handed me his payment, would ignite my private adventures in solitary love.

Sometimes, when his shop wasn't busy, we'd talk. The vibrations of his voice would diffuse through my body when he, with an easy optimism, would tell me of his plans to manufacture his own gems and precious metals rather than import them, the gems from India and the ingots of silver and gold from Spain. Other times he'd speak about his gratitude to Saul for taking him in, teaching him the art and craft of metalworking, and introducing him to the League of Alchemists. They're his family, the men who believe in him and share their secrets with him, secrets he hopes will advance his business and save his clients money.

Just as I was imagining him in every detail—his high-bridged nose and rugged cleft chin, his broad shoulders and chiseled muscles—and just as I was envying his sense of purpose, his freedom to set his own goals, and his self-confidence when making decisions, I was jarred out of my reverie by a crush of scarlet-cloaked soldiers. That jolt and the sour stink fanning out from their pores of last night's henket, an Egyptian beer made from barley or emmer wheat, roused me from my trance and sent me north onto the Street of the Soma toward the agora, which is just east of the Great Harbor's dockyards and warehouses.

The agora, our central marketplace, is both the heart of the city and its cloaca of gossip, the venue for seeing and being seen, for hearing and being heard. Like the legendary agoras in the Greek city-states, ours consists of a series of long, low buildings that face a central plaza, each building or *stoa* fronted by a portico to shade and shelter its shoppers. Within the *stoas* and their adjoining small buildings are shops, *kapeleia* for light snacks, small inns, and industrial workshops.

Its vigor filtered into my lifeless arteries as haranguing hawkers and hucksters, orators and priests, soothsayers and astrologers, tricksters and swindlers, magicians and conjurers, snake charmers and peddlers, wizards and sorcerers all promised me a miracle for a price. Men and women of every class, many in the stunning colors of their native garb, bustled about the stalls, tents, and awning-sheltered barrows. Among them were hordes of slaves, pickpockets, cutthroats, musicians, Oriental dancers, prostitutes, loiterers, and speculators, all accompanied by the din of carts, the haggling of buyers, the calls of tinkers, the blandishments of vendors, the pleas of beggars, the quarrels of men, the gossip of women, and the buzz of flies. I raised my hem to tiptoe around the ripe twists of excrement and the opals of phlegm that dotted the pavement while I confronted the squawks of caged fowl awaiting the butcher's knife, the smoky odors of street food, and the reek of salted meat hanging in strips, threaded with fat, and streaked with blood.

Judah's stall is well situated in the agora, in a *stoa* facing both the center of the marketplace and the Street of the Soma, so his location is always congested with moneychangers' tables and merchants' wagons, the dealers of these portable businesses vying each day for a favorable spot, their disputes sometimes requiring the governor's official to settle. Maneuvering around them to cross the plaza, drenched in liquid sunlight, awash in both the fever of desire and the chill of dread, I forewent a snack of figs and a cheese pastry at my favorite *kapeleion*. Instead, welcoming the shade of his *stoa*'s portico, I dawdled in the neighboring stalls, some for wines, others for Alexandrine glassware, Corinthian bronze statuary, Greek pottery, and Oriental carpets, grateful for the opportunity to tarry while I garnered the courage to enter his stall empty handed.

Chapter 10

Sunday Afternoon

GARNERING THE courage with a few deep breaths, I pinched my cheeks for some color and entered Judah's stall on a spike of sunlight that stretched past his displays of bejeweled gold and silver chains and settled on the scrim that curtains off his living quarters. He was facing the entrance, seated on a stool, arched over his workbench in front of the scrim. Intent on his craft, his sandaled feet resting on the white tile floor, his lips parted, his calloused hands were skillfully weaving strands of metal into a wire gauze for spreading the heat of a flame. Eager to fix this image of him in my memory but ready to look away if he should catch me staring, I must have sighed during a surge of sweet imaginings, because his concentration broke and he raised his lids to look at me with steady eyes.

I felt as though he'd touched me.

"Hello, Miriam."

His voice resonated through my body, triggering such a wave of tremors that I had to grip the edge of one of the stools around his display counter to stop the fluttering of my himation.

But, like my father, he got right to the point.

"Miriam, I was counting on seeing you today. I've been concerned about returning the scrolls before anyone realizes I borrowed them."

One of Homer's Gorgons materialized before me, baring her fangs, seizing me with her terrible gaze, and turning my pale courage to stone.

"The scrolls? Actually I'd quite forgotten about them. I just dropped in to tell you I've designed the apparatus for you and

68

Saul and I'll have everything for you, my design, your scrolls, and the apparatus, by next week."

I forced a tight smile to cover the lie that was burning like acid in my throat.

Raking his hands through his hair, he took several seconds to respond.

"You know, Miriam, I borrowed the scrolls without telling anyone. They still consider you an outsider. Besides, I'd be mortified if Saul notices their absence. As it is, he's afraid our years of hard work could get into the wrong hands. I thought you understood that."

"Saul. How is Saul? Last time I was here you told me he had a cough and was developing a tremor in his hands."

I'd only met Saul twice, once last year when I first started coming to the shop to collect Judah's mortgage payment, and another time more recently when I saw them together at a craft meeting at the Great Synagogue. I'd gone there on the pretext of using its library and happened to buy a scroll about the lives of the women in the *Torah*, but my real purpose was to catch a glimpse of Judah. The prospect of seeing him or hearing his voice, even just his name, brought me pleasure.

When I met Saul, I was struck by his hands, a young man's hands, strong, large but graceful, with long square fingers and oval tapered nails. He's not quite handsome, despite his crest of reddish curls only slightly threaded with gray, but he's tall and broad-shouldered with a kind square face, a wide mouth, and a strong brow.

Judah had told me that Saul's a widower. His wife, Dinah, died a few years ago, but she'd been sick with mania for more than twenty years, since the birth of their only child, a son named Eran. Saul had done everything to ease her suffering, even taking her to the *asclepieion* at Pergamon, the famous healing temple dedicated to Asclepius, the Greek god of health and medicine. There she was treated with a special diet, dream therapy, mineral baths, exercise, and massage along with various healing rituals—one in particular involved sleeping in a dormitory with non-venomous snakes crawling all over the floor—but nothing could restore the balance of her yellow bile. So, when Saul wasn't in the shop, he'd be home taking care of Dinah and Eran, and when he was in the shop, he'd be teaching Judah his craft.

Judah once told me about a regular customer who'd come to the shop to ask Saul to make the wedding ring he'd designed for his fiancée. When Saul called for Judah to assume the project, the man objected, insisting that Saul make the ring himself. Showing him Judah's work, including rings more elaborate than the customer's own design, Saul tried to persuade him that Judah was more than capable of alloying the gold and shaping the metal for the ring. When the customer insisted, Saul refused his business and sent him to another craftsman in the agora.

"Does he still have his cough?" I grabbed this opportunity to change the subject from the scrolls, but I could tell by Judah's momentary squint and the slight turn of his head that I hadn't fooled him.

"His cough persists, along with a shortness of breath when he lies down. That and the tremor make him too sick to continue working on our recipe." His tone was dry, with a trace of impatience.

But then, after a thoughtful pause, he added in a more liquid tone, "If you have time, I could show you samples of the deadened copper he heated with a seed of silver to enhance the spirit of the mercury bath." And, as if he needed to justify spending the time with me after my failure to return the scrolls, he muttered almost to himself, "I take my afternoon break now anyway."

He took a few minutes to rewind his spool of wire, store the metal scraps in an earthenware *cantharus*, a two-handled drinking cup, and wipe his tools. When he stood, the folds of his gray *colobium*, a coarse, woolen workingman's tunic, short-sleeved, cut above the knee, and belted at the waist, relaxed around his torso and whispered across his thighs. The air moved with him as he checked beyond his entrance to make sure no potential clients were approaching his stall. Then he closed and locked the wrought-iron grille but left the heavy wooden shutters open.

When he ushered me into his cubicle, I was struck by its astringent cleanliness and Spartan simplicity. With the few watery slices of light filtering in from the single louvered, east-facing window, I could see the sparse furnishings, only a covered sleeping couch, a washstand and basin, and a table and chair. Two raw pine shelves held a mirror, razor, and comb; a chamber pot; two amphora joined by a knotted rope (for hauling water from the public fountain); a smaller amphora (this one of wine); several ceramic flasks; a bronze oil lamp and shade (with a striker and trimmer); a tallow lamp (and candles); and a portable oil-burning lantern (fitted with a thin sheet of mica to direct the light). He also had some tin crockery and cutlery, a short stack of towels, and a wax tablet and stylus. Attached to the lower shelf were several hooks on which he hung his himation, a leather apron, a tunic of plain bleached linen for *Shabbat* and the holy days, a pair of low boots buckled together, a scroll of the *Septuagint* in an embroidered silk case, and a silver chain with an amulet of a bird in flight.

I was drawn to the amulet.

He followed the sweep of my gaze. "My mother gave me that shortly before she died to remind me of how she'd taught me to live, unencumbered and free of conventions, prejudices, and clutter. Instead, she encouraged me to respect who I am and what I've earned, to value economy and simplicity, and to make commitments sparingly."

The Gorgon retracted her brazen claws and calmed her mane of venomous snakes when Judah entrusted me with that piece of his history.

But I also began to wonder whether he was warning me not to expect a commitment (as if he, not I, were the one betrothed) and whether he'd brought other women to his cubicle (as if he, not I, were the one filled with lust). When and how had I become not only a liar but a Siren ready to shelve all restraint and betray my steadfast and devoted Noah?

Roused from my self-recriminations by his footfalls on the mud bricks that paved his cubicle, I saw that he'd already gathered samples from a few of the flasks and arranged them on the table. When I sat on the chair before them, Judah moved behind me so the feeble light from the window could illuminate the array. Leaning over my shoulder, close enough for me to sense the cloud of sandalwood around him, he pointed to samples, explaining how each represented a step in the deadened copper's transformation.

At that moment, I was absorbed more by the cloud of sandalwood than the samples of copper. Unable to calm my yearnings, let alone concentrate on his explanation, my senses reeling, my heart hammering, my breath quickening, I spun out of the chair intent on escaping the fire raging in my blood.

Only to pitch into his arms.

I remember my confusion, then embarrassment, that a muffled whine escaped from my lips, that he held me, his heat pulsating through me, our hearts pounding in synchrony, that a blush of shyness washed over me while an alarm blared in my ears. He raised my chin and searched my eyes to see whether I'd caught a glimpse of eternity or was merely in the throes of a seizure.

I asked, "Do you love me?" but only with my eyes.

"I'm no good for you, Miriam," he groaned while stepping back. "You were meant for a life I can't give you. You need to go home now, because if I did what I want to do, we wouldn't stop, and before we knew it, you'd have to bear on your wedding night the stigma of this afternoon and maybe even the invectives that were hurled at my mother and me."

His face blurred as my tears welled up, a few trickling down my face, but I caught my breath, leveled my gaze, and squared my shoulders. He turned and advanced toward the shop entrance while I lagged behind to give him just enough time to unlock and open the grille so I could cross the threshold without having to see his beautiful face pinched with pity, irritation, or contempt.

I plunged into the afternoon light, following my shadow this time as it lengthened toward the Jewish Quarter, my thoughts in concert with the thunder of the breakers crashing against the rocks and shoals of Pharos Island. Nevertheless, I vowed that with or without Judah's love, I would become an alchemist to study the spirit of metals and prevent the sickness that comes from working with them, and that no matter what, I would recover the scrolls in time to return them to him next week.

Chapter 11

Late Sunday Afternoon

AFTER THE LOSS of not only the scrolls but the dream of a romance with Judah, I needed the tenderness of a friend. So, rather than return home, I dragged myself the extra blocks to Noah's house even knowing that, of all people, I hardly deserved his sympathy.

Amram was not at home, but their narrow-eyed, bullish doorkeeper, Myron, emerged from his cell off the entryway to squint against the slanting sunlight and identify me through the grid of iron bars that covers the porter's hole in their thick, metal-studded entryway door. Despite the many years since the flames of the Pogrom devoured their family, I couldn't get used to this opulent, almost ostentatious fortress as their home, but I understood it.

After greeting me and taking my himation, Myron escorted me past a dark-skinned, knock-kneed lad sweeping invisible dust into an invisible pile and ushered me to a padded stone bench in the atrium. While I rested alongside its pool of floating lotus blossoms, beds of dark blue irises, and rows of alabaster statues bearing lamps of aromatic oils, he sent for two maids. One placed a bronze footstool under my feet, removed my boots, wiped my feet with a damp towel, and fitted me with a pair of slippers. The other brought me a small mahogany serving table set with a silver chalice, a pitcher of cold water, and a flagon of wine from Palestine.

When I'd refreshed myself, Myron guided me to the courtyard through a maze of spice-scented, marble-columned corridors. We passed rosewood tables bearing urns of fresh rose petals and baskets of lavender, calamus, saffron, and cinnamon; claw-footed cedar chests trimmed with bone; and airy drawing rooms (separate ones for men and women but opening one to the other) with islands of highly varnished, rigidly placed, massive furniture inlaid with tortoiseshell, ivory, and mother-of-pearl.

The corridor led us to an ivy-covered arch through which I saw Noah, his pale body dressed in a tunic of Scythopolitan linen embroidered with a border of russet leaves and belted with a wide leather strap studded with gold coins. Barefoot in the shade of a strawberry tree and surrounded by a hedge of red-flowering hibiscus, he was staring into the eyes of a marble griffin, its open beak spurting water into a circular, turquoise pool. Posed like a marble statue himself, his gaze unyielding, he was leaning forward on a speckled granite bench, his legs crossed at the knees, his left elbow balanced on his thigh, his chin resting on his folded manicured hand.

He looked up to welcome me with the toothy smile he always reserved for me.

"Mimi, how beautiful you look."

Actually, my *tunica interior* was drenched, my chiton askew, my face tear-stained, and my hair bedraggled. The pins that held my braid had come loose so my crown had slipped into a dissolute tilt, and the curls across my forehead hung like limp streamers. Plus, my toes had been cramped all day inside hot leather boots, the shooting pains easing only as the swelling in my feet began to subside. But to my surprise, I no longer cared how I looked to Noah.

I flopped onto the cushioned wrought-iron chair across from him, kicked off the slippers, pulled my knees to my chest, smoothed my chiton over my knees and ankles, and wrapped my arms around my shins. My back to the fountain, a teak table between us, I shaded my eyes with my palm to avoid squinting into the late afternoon sun.

"I was out walking and wanted to see how you were. You left *Shabbat* dinner feeling so sick."

"It was just a headache, Mimi."

Maybe so, but the skin around his jaw tightened, and his body stiffened.

Then I noticed his right hand and arm were bandaged to the elbow.

"Noah, what happened to your arm?"

"On the way home from your house, I was attacked by a pack of hounds. They wanted the grilled lamb. Anyway, once I hurled the food basket, they sprinted after it and left me alone."

"Oh, Noah. Let me make a salve for you and massage it into your arm. Remember how you nursed me through my convalescence from the bee stings?"

"Yes. I also remember how you visited me every day when my mother and sisters were killed. I had only you to comfort me. My father was too distraught, too grief stricken and guilt ridden to realize that he still had a son who'd lost a mother. Only you understood what that loss meant. But, Mimi, the arm is nothing. It's just a little sore."

"Let me at least freshen the bandage."

His eyebrows shot up almost to his hairline.

"No."

"Then let me see how it's heal—"

"No, no, no." He flicked his hand to end the discussion.

He was resisting my attempts to minister to him, and I didn't know why. Not then.

During the silence that grew between us, I heard the ping of glassware and the clink of cutlery as a maid approached balancing a silver tray across her pillowy breasts. Perching the tray on the edge of the table as she covered it with a cloth of bleached Indian cotton, she unfurled a starched napkin for each of us with an efficient snap of her pudgy wrist. Then, unloading the tray, her reddened hands served us grapes and an assortment of cheeses on a gold-leaf platter; two small silver dishes, one of pistachio nuts and the other of mixed berries; a crater of wine; a pair of crystal goblets; some silver utensils; and a cut-glass bowl of floating red roses.

When she'd left, Noah pushed the small dishes together as if to choose one or the other, but instead he plucked the grapes with his long, bony fingers and concentrated on lining them up across the cloth. When he was satisfied with the arrangement, he scooped up a handful of nuts and popped them in his mouth before ladling some wine into a goblet and raising it to his lips. He drained the goblet, and wiping his mouth with the back of his hand, he took measure of me over its rim.

His silence was making me nervous, so I poured a goblet of wine for myself.

"Noah, you were gazing at the fountain as if you'd never seen it before."

He shrugged, and then, sputtering some nut fragments, he spoke to the space above my head.

"I have to find a new scribe to replace Drakon. He's worked long hours without complaint, has a keen memory, and speaks and writes Latin as well as you do, but I've caught him snooping more than once. Just this morning, he was copying my list of prospective clients. As soon as he heard me enter the office, he stopped, and in a stream of rapid prattle, proffered some convoluted excuse for having opened my files."

"Is he the one with the pockmarked face and the wolfish gray teeth who brings documents for Papa to approve? I always sensed something furtive about him."

"Well, never mind him." Noah shrugged his shoulders. "That's only business. How are you, Mimi?" And then lowering his gaze and giving me a long, pointed look, he asked, "What's that gash on your forehead?"

"I fell early this morning on a step in the library." I launched into the story of the missing scrolls and how, in my panic, I'd gouged my forehead on the edge of one of the risers. "I must get those scrolls back, Noah. I feel as though I'm teetering on the edge of an abyss."

He lowered his eyelids, compressed his lips, and shook his head in a narrow arc as if he had the wisdom of Solomon and I had the brain of an imbecile.

"Oh, Mimi. How can you say that? Sometimes you're so melodramatic. Soon we'll be married. We'll have a family. I think our wedding is the only event that can ease my father's grief and restore his health—"

I'd begun to wonder whether Amram's melancholia all these years could have been treated with an extract of mandrake root.

"—He loves you like a father, and I love and yearn for you like an eager bridegroom."

Beads of perspiration began stippling his brow.

"Unless I return those scrolls, and I mean soon, before their absence is noticed, I will live in shame. Not only will I have broken a promise, but should the secret leak out that some Jews are fabricating precious metals and gems, we'll all be at risk for another pogrom."

The beads on his brow were coalescing.

"What bothers me almost as much as their disappearance is that my father or brother would do such a thing. Someone lifted the scrolls between Friday afternoon when I began my preparations for *Shabbat* and early this morning. Papa and Binyamin were the only ones who knew about the scrolls and had a motive and opportunity to take them during that time."

Even Noah, who might have been jealous of my preoccupation with the League, couldn't have taken them. I had personally wrapped him in his himation, escorted him to our door, and watched him until he disappeared around the corner.

He lifted his chin and, with a gusty sigh, rolled his eyes as if pleading to the heavens for patience.

"Oh, Mimi, why would either of them even want the scrolls?"

"They each need money, money that could come from selling them. The secrets would be worth a fortune on the black market. Binyamin needs to finance a voyage to Rome and then a trek to Capua. And my father? I have no idea why he needs the money, but he does, and I intend to get to the bottom of that too."

Noah arched one eyebrow. "Come on, Mimi, don't be so silly. They'll turn up. You're overreacting. I'm sure you've just misplaced them."

His condescension stung me like a lash. Blinking at him in

disbelief, I leaned across the table, close enough to smell his foulness.

And then I pounced on him.

"How can you say such a thing? How dare you say such a thing! How can you be so dismissive of my distress? You know my routines, how meticulously I adhere to them, and you know how important honoring a commitment is to me. I thought you'd be sympathetic, that you'd understand the magnitude of this loss to me."

I couldn't believe how shrill my voice had become. I lifted my goblet to take a sip of wine, but my hands were trembling so much that the wine sloshed over the rim. So I put the goblet down.

By now, his face was slick with sweat, and his narrow shoulders began to shake as if he'd caught a chill.

"What about honoring your commitment to me?" He muttered the question without inflection, his eyes narrowed, his mouth morphing into a mirthless half smile, the edges of his front teeth bared, while he poked a grape with the tip of his knife.

A swell of anger rolled up my spine. My father had made the commitment, not I. And that was when I was too young to understand and the prospect of marriage was more remote than real. Still, Noah was right. I'd been evading the commitment. So I suppressed my flight instinct and sidestepped his bitterness.

"Oh, Noah! What on earth is the matter with you today?"

"I'm amazed, even alarmed, Mimi, that you could be so upset over having misplaced a couple of scrolls belonging to some feckless dreamers, let alone how you could occupy yourself with their nonsense. I've never seen you so frantic. And how could you ever imagine that your father or Binyamin would steal them to sell on the black market?"

"I can think of no other explanation for their disappearance." Ice poured out with my voice. "Papa or Binyamin could and would steal and sell them if desperate enough and didn't realize the consequences."

I refrained from mentioning that my father might have

taken the scrolls simply to discredit me before the League and propel me toward marriage. Little did Papa realize that even death held less sway over me now than the prospect of marrying Noah. I gagged whenever I imagined his toothy kisses; his rolling on top of me, forcing his tumescence inside me, arching his back to penetrate me, grunting and spewing his fetid breath with each thrust; and coating my skin with his foulness before flopping his sticky manhood on my thigh.

Dizziness swept through my hollow belly as I struggled to stand and slide my feet into the slippers. When Noah rushed over—whether to help or divert me, I can't say—I could see that the sweat on his face had congealed into a waxy film and his eyes were glazed with fever.

"Mimi, please. Please don't go. I see I've offended you. I had no idea the scrolls were so dear to you. Please, my most beautiful darling, you must forgive me."

At that moment, I had more important things to do than listen to him gush. I had to deal with my father's urgent need for money and the disappearance of the scrolls. I knew I'd have to deal with the betrothal sooner or later, but now—when I was feeling only a keen desire to hurt him—was hardly the time.

Chapter 12

Monday, Early Morning into Early Afternoon

"ARE YOU READY to go, Phoebe?"

I was helping her on with her *lacerna*, a long, hooded, homespun cloak, her mission being to catch any hint in the early-morning gossip swirling in and about the agora that the scrolls were for sale. I was ready to sell all my jewelry to recover them, even the pieces that had belonged to my mother, except, of course, the Alexandrian pearls, which had been part of her dowry. According to tradition and as specified in our parents' marriage contract, if my mother predeceased my father, then the eldest son would inherit her dowry.

"And you, Miriam?" Phoebe had fastened the fibula to my himation and was stooping to adjust its folds.

I was venturing out early too, but only locally, to get the fruits and herbs to make Papa's favorite salad, anything to allay his defenses while I prodded him with questions.

Phoebe and I were in the atrium. The first pale streaks of daylight were peeping through the *compluvium*, the open circle in the roof above the pool. They spun a soft gray glow on the water and edged the walls in silver. After checking our reflection in the pool's glassy surface, we plunged into the morning chill. As we parted at the corner of our two streets and she made her way west, I listened until I could no longer hear her footsteps and then turned eastward.

I'd forgotten the sounds of the awakening city: the moan of the surf ebbing and resurging, the faint toll of the buoys, the steady throb of legionnaires' hobnail boots, the distant growl of waking dogs, and the rumble of produce-laden carts passing through the city's gates. The raw scent of the sea hung in the greasy air as I dragged my shadow through the still-deserted streets. Wending my way toward the local plaza, I passed the stable yards and villas of the most affluent Jews, their columned entrances adorned with carved architraves imported from Libya and Asia, their citron-scented gardens filled with whimsical statuary cavorting under arcs of jetting water. Their manicured lawns behind walls of box and rosemary and their crushed-shell walkways gave way to shoddy, sun-scoured, mud-brick tenements jammed together with hardly a slice of sky between them. Pigeons roosted above their listing doorways, squirting excrement on their crumbling lintels while their shutters stayed latched against the dramas of the night.

As I approached the plaza, the rising sun splashed color on the rectangles of silver and slate, and the long shadows resolved into familiar sights. Skirting eddies of trash whirling with the wind and sidestepping dozing idlers slumped against sun-bleached shacks, I spied a hunchbacked beggar wading through heaps of stagnant garbage in a rubbish-strewn alley and a knot of drunks squabbling with a rush of doves over a handful of spilled barley. I heard horses nickering and an old woman humming as she mopped the dusty pavement in front of her shop, and I caught the pungent scent of tethered animals before I saw them switching their tails against the swarms of hovering flies.

Nestor, our produce vendor, stood by the curb in front of his cart, his sturdy body crammed into his *colobium*, the skirt rippling across his meaty thighs, the flesh of his neck folded in tiers over its collar. His thickly corded arms strained the sleeves as he brushed the sweat-lathered coat of his mule and crooned a melody of praise to the beast.

"Good morning, Miss bat Isaac. You're looking more like your beautiful mother each day. How are you and your blessed father this morning?" His lilting voice gushed with gratitude. Before I was born, my father had financed the purchase of Nestor's first cart and mule. Then, at the time of the Pogrom, when all the businesses in the Jewish Quarter failed, my father forgave the balance of the debt. Nestor never forgot my father's generosity.

"It's just for my father that I'm here this morning, to buy the ingredients for his favorite salad: mangoes, kiwis—"

"Oh, I know what he likes, Miss Miriam. Also oranges and raspberries, right? And some crushed mint leaves too. Your beautiful mother made it for him all the time. How could I forget either of your parents?"

Raising his bushy eyebrows and tapping his forehead with his thick, bent index finger, his weathered cheeks broke into creases of cheer around his rosy nose.

He filled my basket and then handed it to me. "Only the freshest ingredients for Mr. ben Asher and his daughter."

As we exchanged good wishes, I pressed a coin into his palm and was on my way.

By now the plaza was coming alive. Peddlers were hawking over the screech of wheels, the clatter of hooves, and the shouts of a gathering crowd. Orbits of activity had replaced the calm of a few minutes ago. The sun stroked my face and glinted off the mica-flecked cobblestones as I shouldered my way through the human river. Sedan chairs bobbed around me as I passed wobbly stands and shabby stalls where the aroma of fresh bread mixed with the scent of men at work. Other drunks and idlers had claimed the outskirts of the plaza, but the hunchbacked beggar was still in his alley. His twisted body now supine on a pile of rubbish, his restless hands scratched at his filthy tunic and greasy hair while a stray sunbeam teased his eyelids. The remaining sunbeams hammered down on my basket while I trudged the last few blocks, at last turning our corner absorbed by the prospect of news from Phoebe.

I KNEW PHOEBE would hardly be racing home with the scrolls. Still, while the morning hours dragged a bloated sun above the trees in the courtyard, that very hope would flash through me. I'd picture her skipping with glee, the hood of her *lacerna* wagging behind her, the breeze wafting wavelets of her dark hair, a dew of perspiration across her brow, and above all, the scrolls secure in her arms. That hope would advance to an expectation whenever I heard footfalls beyond the thicket, even though she'd likely approach our house from the west rather than from the north via our side street.

In the meantime, I was either slumped forward on the edge of the lounge picking at my cuticles or circling the fountain, pounding my fists against my thighs, digging my nails into my palms, and stifling a shriek that, when audible, sounded like the high-pitched whine of a mosquito in orbit around my ear.

I'd long since taken more than the necessary care to make the salad for Papa. I'd loaded the fruits into a wire basket and lowered them into our well to chill. Then I washed them, removed any pits, seeds, and peels, and cut the larger fruits into bite-size pieces. Next I sliced Phoebe's date nut bread into wedges just the way he likes it, and setting aside the uneven pieces and slices, I arranged the rest: the fruit in a cut-glass bowl, each piece flanked by one of a contrasting color, and four wedges of bread precisely stacked in a rattan basket, which I covered with a starched linen napkin.

So immersed was I in the fantasy of returning the scrolls to Judah that I started when I heard Phoebe shuffle into the courtyard. At first I could read nothing but fatigue in her sagging shoulders, but then her eyelids fluttered, her breath expanded into a sigh, and her words spilled out in a hollow voice and a stream of tears.

My Phoebe had been everywhere, beginning with the Public Records Office inside the Palace of Justice, where municipal slaves archive public documents and, as a sideline and for a fee, secure personal documents. Then she'd gone to the soup kitchens, laundry lofts, smithies, and slave dealers' sheds. She'd eavesdropped outside barber shops and bath houses, taverns and whorehouses, cookshops and *kapeleia*, inns and bakers' stalls, and at the scores of dice games and money changers' tables in the agora. She'd listened to the conversations of citizens and freedmen, soldiers and stevedores, peddlers and artisans, masons and mule drivers, slaves and serfs before the midday heat wrapped the streets in silence. Nothing. Either the scrolls had yet to reach the streets, or they weren't for sale.

Relief and despair clutched me in turn, but I still had hope of learning something when I'd present the fruit salad to Papa.

Chapter 13

Monday Afternoon

"PAPA, I BROUGHT you something, your favorite fruit salad to have with Phoebe's date nut bread."

I placed the bowl and basket on his desk so their handles were aligned.

"Miriam, you remind me so much of your mother."

We were in his study again, the same scent of roses sweeping in from the courtyard and the same breeze billowing and snapping the drapes. But this time, unlike Friday, I sat tall before his massive desk, pretending that ropes connected to a block and tackle were pulling my head and shoulders toward the ceiling. My father was studying the accounts he held with Amram, his brow pulled down in concentration, his index finger sliding down a column of numbers, his bronze pen borrowing its glitter from a stripe of sunlight. Standing next to his desk was his abacus, an antique marble-topped table marked with parallel lines and intersecting perpendicular grooves.

"How's business, Papa?" I was angling for a way to broach the subject of our household finances.

"Fine, Miriam, just fine. Noah's participation in our partnership is bringing us unexpected prosperity. I need not remind you that, aside from the fact that his family has considerable wealth, Noah himself is a shrewd investor. You must be the envy of every maiden in the quarter."

"Papa, you know we agreed to postpone any discussion of Noah until the end of the week. Why do you keep bringing him up?" Determined to keep the mounting exasperation out of my voice, I raised my chin and twitched the briefest smile.

His face had hardened to stone, but I could hear his agitation in the rattling of his pen as he set it down on his desk. He waited several seconds before answering.

"Because I'm embarrassed. That's why. I've run out of excuses to give my long-suffering friend. I've told him that your body, like your mother's, is not yet mature enough to bear children, that you need to see Binyamin settled, that Aunt Hannah needs you, that your astrologer needs more time to divine an auspicious date. In short, I've told him everything but the truth, that you're preoccupied with these alchemists and, for all I know, with that bastard jeweler in the agora. I curse the day I ever sent you to collect his mortgage payment."

I blinked at him while dust particles danced in the stripes across his face and a stream of bile swirled in my belly.

"Speaking of payments, Papa, didn't you tell Phoebe that we have to economize? That we need to practice thrift when purchasing our provisions, that we should go to the *pantopoleion* instead of our usual vendors?"

"That's absurd!"

Three vertical furrows cut a fan between his eyebrows as he slammed his fist on the desk, upsetting the basket of bread and causing the bowl of fruit salad to skitter across the table and teeter on the edge before crashing to the floor.

The silence gathered, seeping into every cranny of his study until broken by the flutter of pigeons in the peristyle.

"Did Phoebe tell you that? Has she nothing better to do than spin tall tales? That girl should be scourged."

I wrapped my arms around my chest to contain the fury rumbling through me.

But then he sighed, spread out his palms, and pleaded with me in a muted tone.

"Why are you questioning me about our finances? Haven't I always given you the best?"

Flames of duplicity spread across his fleshy face and down his barrel-shaped neck.

Weary of his dodgery and the smell of his lies, I waggled my head and flicked my hand to fend off this latest ploy to put me on the defensive. If he'd stoop to manipulate me, then he'd lie to my face and steal behind my back. Still, his motive for taking the scrolls was obscure to me. Was it to advance my marriage to Noah? Was this pressure for me to marry based on Papa's embarrassment over the delay, or on something more, like the imminent financial collapse of our family?

I leaned over the desk but kept the anger in my voice under control.

"I've always thought of us as partners in running this household. It's true that you make the business decisions, but I've been the mistress of this household for years, just as Mother was, defining the routines, directing the staff, scheduling our purchases, planning the menus, welcoming our guests, and performing righteous acts. Why would you go to Phoebe about our budget? And more astonishing, why would you yourself go to Moshe to place an order?"

He faced me with the look of a wounded animal, but I held fast to my courage and continued.

"I'm sorry you've been embarrassed in your relationship with Amram. Truly I am, and we can discuss that on Friday, but I too have been embarrassed as your partner in running this household. Moreover, I'm worried that something under this roof is so terribly amiss that you've acted without consulting me and continue to evade the issue with me even now."

The only response was the metallic cry of a gull circling the courtyard.

It seemed pointless to ask him about the scrolls, to give him yet another opportunity to either lie or scold me for being preoccupied with foolishness while neglecting my duty to Noah and our families. So, with nothing more to say, I prepared to leave, this time without requesting permission and without hurrying.

On the contrary, I stalled. I edged out of the chair, heaved a sigh, stretched out my arms, and cupped my knees before lifting myself out of the chair, shaking out the skirt of my tunic and smoothing its folds, hoping he would change his mind and confide in me. When he didn't, I turned toward the atrium, looking back from the mahogany doors but once to see his face twisted in a grimace. His was holding his head in his hands, the heels of his palms pressed against his temples like a vise, as if he were mending a crack in his skull. I realized then that I would have to unearth the answers myself, why he needed money and whether he took the scrolls, even if Charon had to ferry me across the River of Pain to do it.

Chapter 14

Late Monday Afternoon

"MISS MIRIAM, A messenger delivered this letter to you while you were with your father. He said it was urgent."

One of our maids had been waiting for me in the atrium. I'd been about to look for her, to ask her to clean up the shards of glass and the fruit salad swimming on the floor of Papa's study.

The moment she handed me the thin tube inscribed with my name, I recognized the clarity and evenness of Judah's upright penmanship and the simplicity and elegance of his seal. Curling my hand around my neck to check the rising blush, I wondered what news he could be sending me. Had he himself chanced upon the scrolls? As much as I longed for their recovery, I knew I'd drown in shame for the rest of my life if he'd happened upon them.

Suddenly wet, my fingers were almost too slippery to unfurl the papyrus.

> *Miriam,*
>
> *Saul's condition has worsened. I am going to him now. Please meet me there. He lives in the tenement closest to the public fountain on the lane behind The Flamingo's Tongue. Go to the apothecary shop and ask for his landlady, Aspasia.*
>
> *Judah*

My shoulders sagged with relief, but when I imagined Saul

slipping into unconsciousness, his cheeks either hollowed to the bone or swollen with infection, I slumped against the bench, dropped my head, and shut my eyes in shame and then indelible sorrow.

I called out to Phoebe. She scurried in from the kitchen still holding the tray of hard-boiled eggs and goat cheese drizzled with honey that the cook had cobbled together for my father's lunch.

"Please run to a livery stable outside the quarter and hire a sedan chair for me while I put together a basket of food and some medicinal herbs. I need to rush to an apartment in the *Bruchium* Quarter. The bearers of a chair for hire will know the backstreets there. Find a pair we don't know so no one can report to Papa that I've gone to see Judah, and have them meet me around the corner."

Her eyes widened and her jaw dropped. "You're going to meet Judah at his apartment?"

"No. It's not that. Saul is sick, I suspect dying. I need to help Judah. Hurry!" I could have forestalled any gossip by taking her with me, but I wanted to go alone and indulge in the hope that Judah would tell me he loved me.

By the time I'd gathered some willow, garlic, and fennel, wrapped a few bandages, and packed everything in a basket with the remaining fruit salad and date nut bread, Phoebe had returned with the sedan chair and come inside to whisper that the bearers were waiting for me around the corner. Planting herself in front of me, holding me by the elbows, she spun me around in a proprietary check to see that none of the spilled fruit had stained my tunic. Next she draped my himation over my crown of braids to veil the sides of my face. After a hug, she let me go, handing me the basket and waving good-bye with an index finger pressed to her lips.

I passed beneath our portico and circled around to the side street. Hanging in the western sky, the orange sun cast a prickly shadow of me against the thicket that shields our courtyard. Just ahead I met the oily, calculating eyes of a tall, ferret-faced Greek. He must have been the lead bearer because when I recited

Judah's directions to him, he measured me with his eyes, scratched his head with dirt-rimmed fingernails, pursed his lips, drew his eyebrows together, and looked up as if searching for a sign in the sky. Then, nodding, he lowered his gaze and stunned me with the fare. I must have blanched, but with no time to haggle, I readily counted the small bronze coins into his cupped palm. The other bearer was compact with round eyes set in a chinless, ruddy face framed by a tangle of dark fringe flaked with dandruff. He handed me a soiled cushion still bearing the sweaty imprint of the last patron and ushered me with a courtly bow to a tattered wicker chair mounted between two stout bamboo rails and shaded by a sun-bleached, leather parasol. He must have seen me hesitate when my gaze caught the iron fittings lacy with rust, but I offered no resistance when he seated me. Then they lifted me above the glistening pavement and whisked me across the Way. We passed a few legionnaires parched by the sun, propped against each other with an intimacy shared by only soldiers and drunks, and a one-legged beggar. He was slouched against a pillar dozing under its portico, his crutch cast aside, his arms splayed, his neck slack, his head lolled to one side, his mouth agape.

We soon left behind the *Bruchium* Quarter's marble, granite, and limestone townhouses, their pitched roofs tiled, their porticoes decorated with ornamental lamp stands, their gardens carpeted with rose petals, and their grand entrances perfumed with baskets of spices and freestanding pots of clipped rosemary. That neighborhood gave way to rows of claustrophobic buildings faced with faux marble, their roofs flat, their tawdry ground-floor shops shuttered against the pitiless sun, the smell of sewage, and the buzz of flies. Given the swelter of the nearly deserted backstreets and the bearers' brisk rocking rhythm—the compact one had a rolling gait—I myself could have dozed had I not been so preoccupied with both the thrill of seeing Judah and the dread of finding Saul shrouded in pain. Images of the latter churned up a queasiness I could hardly suppress even with repeated swallows.

The bearers, moons of sweat under their armpits, their

bodies glossy, their faces flushed, their hair matted, and their veins thick as cables, set me down by the public fountain in front of Aspasia's apothecary shop. This time I planted a large bronze coin in the lead bearer's grime-scored palm as well as a smaller one in the other's before asking them to wait for me no matter how long. If they would, I promised to pay them double the fare for my return home. Again the lead bearer—his name was Telamon—searched the sky for a sign but now only briefly before nodding, from which I inferred that I could expect them to wait an hour but no more.

I turned around a few times to scan the neighborhood from a ground-level perspective. Shops and saloons, inns and restaurants, tenements and warehouses, lumberyards and stables, factories and grain bins all jostled for space along the shoulders of the narrow lanes. Here, in this the western end of the *Bruchium* Quarter, the brooding odors of the *Rhakotis* Quarter, especially those of the canal that connects the *Kibotos* to Lake Mareotis, permeate the invisible boundary between the quarters to compound the stench from the putrefying garbage heaped behind every saloon, inn, and restaurant along the waterfront.

The muffled commotion of the harbor and the remote but steady rasp of soldiers' hobnail boots were the only sounds to rupture the afternoon quiet until I heard an insistent hiss, the tone too harsh to be the wind rustling the dry grass and the pitch too high to be the slap of the tide. It was Drakon. He'd just staggered out of a saloon and must have spotted me about to cross his path. In the next instant, he was leaning into me, his head thrust forward, his pockmarked face twisted with hatred. As he pulled back his lips to speak, I saw only the peaks of his pointed gray teeth against the dark cavity that was his wicked mouth.

"You imperious busybody." His eyes glittered with fury as he sputtered out his words in a spray of yellow spittle that stung my face.

"It was you, you spiteful Jew-bitch, who got your mealy-mouthed, foul-smelling boyfriend to fire me! But I'll show you both. The Emperor himself has appointed me head scribe to the new prefect of Judea. So off to Caesarea I'll go, where I'll be glad to stir up trouble against the likes of you and your smarmy race."

With that and a smirk, he swept the air with his hand as if to show the world he'd gotten the better of me. Then he turned on his heel and stalked across the street, but not before knocking down a stack of wood in front of the lumberyard.

As if I cared. As if no one had ever hurled an anti-Semitic insult at me before.

I stood rooted for a few moments until the day's second wave of queasiness subsided and then swiveled my head to see who might have overheard him. Not even the bearers were about. So, with a deep breath, I continued to survey the neighborhood. The other tenements clustered around the fountain were, like Saul's, five or six stories high and fronted by shops. When I knocked on the closed shutters of the apothecary shop, a frail-boned old woman with a pleated mouth and liquid blue eyes squinted through the slats. Opening the shutters against the blazing daylight, she was still gripping the long wooden key she'd used to unlock the grille, perhaps to have it handy as a makeshift club.

But she'd been expecting me. Stepping aside and ushering me in with a wave of her knotted hand and a sympathetic pat on my shoulder, she explained that she needed but a minute to belt her tunic—it was vermillion, probably dyed with red cinnabar—and exchange her slippers for sandals. Sidling past bundles of herbs that hung from her ceiling on ropes, she ducked behind the wicker screen at the back of her shop, giving me some time to appreciate the orderly arrangement of her inventory and test myself on the use of each herb and tonic, seed and powder, paste and unguent, preparation and mixture as Hector had taught me.

A waist-high wooden bench spanned the warped floorboards at the center of her shop. I could see from the pyramid of crushed cannabis leaves on its marble top and an open scroll of *De Medicina* that she'd been compounding suppositories to relieve the pain of hemorrhoids. With the sunlight streaming through the open shutters, I could read on neatly printed labels the contents of each amphora, ceramic jar, and alabastron on the tower of shelves near her bench. She stocked the usual: castor oil, figs, and white hellebore for constipation; opium for pain, diarrhea, and insomnia; aloe for rashes; crocodile dung and sour milk to blend for a contraceptive; and various animal fats to combine for treating baldness. Those were just some of the remedies I recognized.

And then, on a polished porphyry counter that spanned the front of the shop, she displayed racks of double-handled greenish glass vials containing her own formula for a mouth rinse and her own chewable breath sweetener, probably made from natron. I was tempted to buy the mouth rinse and breath sweetener for Noah, but I knew he'd be embarrassed so I didn't.

Aspasia emerged in a minute or two. Aside from having donned a pale blue silk belt and leather sandals tied with ribbons to match, she'd tucked in the unruly strands that had escaped from the yellowish-white braid that straggled down her back and painted her lips with an oil of red ochre. As a healer and businesswoman, she knew the importance of a vital appearance, but to me her reddened lips changed her from a healthful looking older woman into a sickly looking younger one.

As I walked out to the street, she relocked the grille and closed the shutters. I followed her stooped shoulders and sweeping braid around the corner of the building through a walkway so narrow I instinctively turned sideways, until we reached a closed door toward the rear of the building. There she uttered a guttural rebuke to subdue the snarling mongrel that was chained to guard the entrance. Perhaps it was straining against its collar because it sensed the hammering of my heart and the quickening of my breath, but I was seized by only an unbearable longing to see Judah, an impatience that was flooding my chest like the incoming tide. The mangy beast kept glowering at me, but it hushed its bark and did little else to challenge me.

Aspasia led me into a dark stairwell that reeked from its

own ripe combination of urine, fried fish, henket, and something else I couldn't identify. The smell intensified as I followed her hem up the steep, twisting staircase to the second-floor hallway, where she left me alone to knock on Saul's door.

Chapter 15

Early Monday Evening

I CALMED MYSELF with a few of my now-routine deep breaths before knocking on the door, but Judah opened it before I could touch my knuckles to the scarred wood.

"Miriam, I knew you'd come."

For a moment nothing existed but his luminous green eyes.

Then he beckoned me in and took my basket. If he was surprised I came alone, he didn't show it.

"I brought some food and a few medicines. I didn't know what Aspasia would have in stock."

"Having you here gives me some hope, but I know he's very sick."

I leaned forward to hear him. His words, thick with sadness, sounded as if they'd passed through a long, dry tube.

When he reached for my himation to hang on a hook by the door, I wanted to press his hands in mine, but I checked the impulse. Later I was sorry. It would have seemed so natural.

"Where is Saul now?"

"He's resting in his *cubiculum*." Judah tilted his head toward the curtain. "The boy's been watching him. At least for the moment, Saul can breathe lying down, and he's not spattering so much blood when he coughs."

I knew that kind of cough could be symptomatic of acute mercury poisoning, that he'd inhaled the vapors from the mercury bath. Still, his breathing had improved. That was a good sign. Maybe his lungs were clearing.

But after a pause, Judah added, "My biggest concern is his tremors. His hands shake and his face twitches, mostly at the

97

corners of his mouth. The twitching has gotten worse, extending now to his eyelids, lips, and tongue. He can't even feed himself. He can't hold a spoon, and as if that weren't bad enough, his mouth is so full of sores his teeth are falling out."

That's when I knew Saul was teetering between life and death, that he was suffering as well from a chronic form of mercury poisoning, that he could die in the throes of a delirium like David and Uri.

I couldn't think of anything comforting to say, but I didn't have to. After a shared silence, Judah continued.

"Sometimes his face stiffens and reddens as if flooded by a fountain of lava. His nostrils flare in a fit of recollected rage directed at his son Eran, who disowned him years ago. After a series of rows, Eran stormed out of their house and left Alexandria for good. Saul howls as long as he can gasp for breath, and then a silence more frightening than his piteous wails settles over him like a dark gas."

Judah's squint and hard blinks told me he was fighting back tears. So I shifted our conversation.

"Has Saul's physician been here today?"

"He was here this morning. He recommends bloodletting. He says Saul's been coughing up blood because there's too much of it in his chest. But Saul's already so weak from the tremors that I'm afraid to let the physician bleed him. That's why I wanted your opinion."

"Well, bloodletting isn't the only treatment for too much blood in his chest. Another is to use tourniquets to trap the blood in the extremities, to prevent the blood from flowing into the chest. The tourniquets should be tied—but not too tightly—around each arm near the shoulder and around each leg just below the groin. I'll take a look at Saul to see whether I think he should be treated with tourniquets or bloodletting, and maybe we can relieve his other symptoms, at least temporarily."

The sound from Judah's throat was so faint I couldn't be sure he'd even spoken.

Only then did I look around and realize we were still standing at the open door of Saul's front room. Far from being dingy like the hallway, the room was clean, tidy, and comfortably furnished with a sideboard, two carved ebony dining couches, and a pair of well-worn occasional chairs that faced each other across a low mahogany table, its surface inlaid with ivory. Enough of the fading sunlight slanted through the window to polish the white tile floor and paint panels of afternoon light on the frescoed walls. Some flashes glanced off the silver, gold, and bronze bowls, pitchers, goblets, trays, and candelabra displayed about the room, all the work of a master craftsman in his prime.

Judah closed the door and walked me past the kitchen toward Saul's *cubiculum*, his hand following but not quite touching the small of my back. Here the odor of the dying overpowered the scent of sunlight, but I resisted the impulse to cover my nose. When Judah pulled aside the curtain, instead of Saul, I saw a translucent, barely breathing, rail-thin cadaver twitching on a sleeping couch covered with sour linen spattered with arcs of dried blood. His hairline had receded; even his reddish curls had thinned to a tangle of grayish tufts. His face was covered with a smear of stubble, and his eyes had sunken into dark rings. Strands of spittle trailed from the lipless hole that used to be his mouth but was now a toothless hollow lined with open sores, trickles of dried blood, and a crust of greenish mucous.

Near him crouched a table jammed with the paraphernalia of the sick: vials of herbs, alabastra of scented oils, stacks of bandages to absorb his blood and spittle, and a copy of the *Septuagint*. I knelt at his bedside first with my lips to his forehead, next with my fingers on his pulse, and then with my ear to his chest. If he was aware of a consoling presence, his gave no sign. His red-lined lids would flutter open, but his face remained expressionless. When he'd utter a grunt, the sound was faint, like an echo from the World-to-Come.

All the while Judah stood in the shadows with a haggard face, fingering his amulet, his other arm around an impossibly skinny boy with the beginnings of a mustache above his thick upper lip. I recited the *Sh'ma*, our declaration of faith in the One G-d, and then asked Him to accept my holiness and direct me to a treatment for Saul.

When I asked for a basin of water and some fresh towels and bedding, Judah gave the boy a pat and off he went thumping down the steps two at a time.

We waited, listening together to the quiet.

I COVERED SAUL with a fresh sheet and washed him, taking care to remove the dried blood and mucous without opening the sores around his mouth. After that, Judah lifted and held him while I remade the bed. Finally, I massaged Saul's back and elbows with a lavender-scented oil and gathered the soiled linen for the boy to take away.

Then, after a nod toward Judah, we tiptoed back to the front room.

"Yes, Judah," I said after we'd taken seats across from each other on the occasional chairs. We were leaning toward one another, Judah's elbows resting on his thighs, his hands dangling over his knees, his face numbed by sadness. "In my opinion, Saul's too weak for a bloodletting. He has no fever, but his heartbeat is faint. The most we should do is use tourniquets to ease his cough."

Judah lowered his chin to his chest and raked his hands through his thicket of curls.

"Still," I said, "we can treat him with garlic to stabilize his breathing and cannabis tea to strengthen his heartbeat and relax his tremors."

He shrugged and then nodded, his palms curled open, his eyes closed.

I walked to the window to verify that the bearers were still there. Then I turned to him. "Let's be grateful that Saul is not suffering now. With the garlic and cannabis tea, we can keep him comfortable. I'll leave the basket with you. Aspasia can bring you whatever else you need. Send for the physician to apply the tourniquets if Saul begins to cough up blood again. I must go now, but know that you'll both be in my daily prayers."

Judah heaved a sigh, got up, and sighed again, this time with an even deeper sadness. He fetched my himation, walked me into the hallway, and led me down the steps and past the dog, who growled at me again but this time only softly. Guiding me with his arm draped lightly around my waist—I slowed my walk to ease into his embrace—he waited for Telamon to get up from his squat and claim me. Then he squared his shoulders and followed me with his eyes as he waved good-bye.

Chapter 16

Monday Night

THE MIDNIGHT darkness was pressing against my sitting room windows with only the feeble light of a flickering candle drifting in from my *cubiculum* and a fragile moon printing the crowns of cypress trees on the mosaic floor. Phoebe had been pacing back and forth between the cushioned mahogany armchairs and the matching sofa where I sat. Then she'd loop around my marble-topped wicker writing desk and its armless chair, careful, of course, not to shift any of the perfectly aligned ovoid rocks I displayed there.

Muttering through compressed lips, she'd been waggling her head, blinking furiously, and shaking an extended index finger as if upbraiding an intractable child when she stopped abruptly and turned to grasp my hands.

"Please, Miriam. You must not go out tonight."

I was taken aback by the fierceness in her voice.

"I have to go, Phoebe. I heard Papa tell his bearers to be ready with his sedan chair again tonight."

"But the streets are dangerous, Miriam. You heard what happened to Levi's neighbor when he went into the *Rhakotis* Quarter. He's still in a coma, and he went there in broad daylight. You're going out in the dead of night, and for all you know, you could end up there too."

My hands hurt, she was squeezing them so hard.

"I suspect Papa's been frequenting a pricey courtesan. So, I doubt if he'll be haunting the slums." If not to a courtesan, then where else could he be going so late at night and spending so much money?

102

"You know there's no safe place in Alexandria at night. At least take your father's bodyguard." She'd stepped back and dropped her chin, but too late to hide the color that was flooding her face and the tears that were welling up in her eyes. Still she kept her grip on my hands.

"Phoebe, I can't. He reports to my father, and I can't risk Papa's finding out that I'm spying on him. Then I'd never discover why he needs money, and he'd be so indignant he'd never forgive let alone recover from the insult."

"What about taking Binyamin with you, or better yet, sending him instead?"

"I can't risk that either. That's all we'd need, another excuse for Binyamin to needle Papa. Besides, it's none of Binyamin's business. It's only become my business because Papa depends on me to run this household."

A grave intensity clouded her childlike face.

"Don't worry, Phoebe. Just bring me your *lacerna*. I can hide my body in its full mantle and bury my face in its deep hood."

Staring through the wide, arched windows at the shapes of varying darkness, I continued to question my decision to follow Papa. Had my curiosity gone amok, or was Athena herself empowering me? Whether or not she'd protect me, whether or not her owl would guide me, I knew I had no choice. How else could I find anything out? Since Papa was too ashamed to admit that we needed to economize, let alone to explain why, he'd be too proud to confess to taking the scrolls, even if his intention had been as benign as redirecting me from Judah and alchemy to Noah and marriage.

And why was he pressing so hard for the marriage now? Noah's interest was showing no sign of waning. Was it only Papa's embarrassment or could it also be that he was facing financial ruin, a calamity that a speedy marriage to Noah could mask if not avert? Noah and his father would accept me not only without a dowry, but they'd extend any and all financial support to my family as if it were their own.

Looking back, I'm not sure why I coupled the loss of the scrolls with Papa's troubles. Perhaps because my awareness of each followed one upon the other so closely. Perhaps because both were shrouded in mystery and the sale of the scrolls could so conveniently restore Papa's solvency. But if Papa did intend to sell the scrolls on the black market, then why hadn't word of them reached the streets?

I needed answers, and I needed them in a hurry. I had fewer than four days till *Shabbat*, fewer than four days to recover the scrolls so I could return them to Judah on Sunday, and fewer than four days till I was due to thrash out with Papa the date of my marriage to Noah.

I was still pondering these questions when a ghost-like reflection of Phoebe appeared in one of the windows.

"Here, take these," she said when I turned to face her.

In addition to her *lacerna*, she'd brought me a portable lantern and a bundle of sesame cakes wrapped in vine leaves. "Be careful," she said. "You can shield the lantern in the folds of the *lacerna*, but if the bearers carry your father into a winding alleyway, or worse yet into a backstreet haunted by drunken derelicts or half-starved dogs, turn around at once and come home. I'll be waiting for you right here."

I could feel her shoulders, now bowed, trembling as she enveloped me first in her *lacerna* and then in her cushioned embrace before handing me the lantern and bundle of sesame cakes.

"And one more thing," she said with an unusual semblance of confidence. She reached behind her back and pulled out a silver-handled carving knife. "Tuck this under your belt. Just in case. You're a Roman citizen. You have the right to defend yourself."

Then it was time. Papa's bearers were calling for him in the atrium. Any sense of security I might have gained from Athena evaporated as soon as I heard their brittle voices. After a few deep breaths to loosen the knot in my belly, I opened the center window against the night chill and sprang to the ground. Clearing the bed of chrysanthemums, I landed inside the arbor, its air dank, its leaves oily, its ceiling a seamless vault of arching shrubs, trees, and vines shielding a secretive world stirred by only the swoop of a bat, the scamper of mice, the call of an owl, or the shriek of its prey. Disoriented, scrabbling through its tunnels, dog-paddling against the leaves to find an opening to the night sky that could point me toward the street, I caught a glimpse of the sedan chair as it was heading toward the *Bruchium* Quarter and spotted the perpetual fire atop the lighthouse.

The fire burned like a brilliant star in the northwestern sky. On the eastern tip of Pharos Island, standing sentinel over the Great Harbor, the lighthouse is our most imposing landmark. The tallest building after the two Great Pyramids of Khufu and Khafra, Antipater of Sidon named it one of the Seven Wonders of the World. A tapering white stone tower, the Pharos Lighthouse reaches almost four hundred feet into the heavens and is visible, some claim, for a hundred miles.

Having withstood the ravages of storms and earthquakes for more than three hundred years, the lighthouse comforted me as I trailed behind the bearers, ducking under porticoes and behind colonnades, scuttling from monument to monument, and otherwise wedging myself behind statuary and topiary. Inasmuch as it would be hours before the city gates would re-open for the peddlers from the countryside to trek in with their goods, the streets were still. The only sounds were the chirr of insects, the occasional voice of a distant ship, and the beat of the bearers' boots against the pavement. Constellations must have salted the sky, but all I remember once we left the torch-lined Canopic Way was a flawless darkness relieved by only the shaft of light from each bearer's hand lamp.

AFTER AN HOUR or so, we branched off the main grid of the *Bruchium* Quarter. Passing a few more warehouses, we entered a knot of narrow, tenement-fringed lanes punctuated by shuttered shops and boarded-up street stalls. We were near the *Rhakotis* Quarter, judging by the shoulder-to-shoulder, ramshackle buildings, the swarm of skeletal cats on the prowl for a water rat, and the position of the lighthouse, now slightly to the east in the northern sky. The fungoid stench of the canal confirmed my estimate. At the same time, the appetite of the mosquitoes reminded me to draw into Phoebe's hood.

My father must have given the bearers a signal, because the sedan chair stopped in front of a ground-floor apartment, giving me the chance to sneak up and crouch behind a fountain caked with pigeon excrement. The apartment looked as if it had been converted into a now-abandoned wine shop, its ancient entrance sealed with cobwebs and a pair of rickety wooden shutters. When one of the bearers knocked, the rusty hinges groaned in protest and the slats shed a shower of silvery splinters. A nightmarish creature with a coffin-shaped head unbolted the door immediately, as if he'd been standing just inside the grime-streaked entrance. After raking each bearer's face with the beam of his lantern, he hobbled toward my father and, with his long, leathery fingers, handed him an amphora of Negrito, a respectable grade of dark red wine.

And then they were off again, with me emerging on cramped legs, dropping behind, picking my way around the potholes, rubble, and clumps of prickly weeds. Or sidling around a tree limb torn loose by the wind. Or pressing myself against a crumbling wall of mud bricks that was the facade of a tenement. Or dodging rubbish as it was thrown out of an upper-story window. Or worse yet, getting splattered by the contents of a chamber pot. A few minutes later, we arrived at a sleazy saloon squatting on the corner of an alley, its face also shuttered. The bearers carried the sedan chair to the back of the saloon, where I saw an oblong of light that was the open door.

Chapter 17

Late Monday Night

WHILE THE BEARERS were depositing Papa, I claimed a vantage point behind a garbage heap opposite the light-filled doorway. The bearers settled around the corner in the alley alongside the saloon, where I could hear their banter, even an occasional raspy guffaw, before their voices sank into a rhythm of phlegmy snores.

Only then did I dare raise my head to peer into the belly of the saloon and match the rattles, jingles, and rumble of voices to an image. A dozen ruffians, one more grotesque than the other, sat with Papa around a well-lit table courting their luck with each throw of the dice and toss of a coin. One among them sat facing the door, a beefy slab of a man with a club at his side. I named him the Enforcer because when he spoke, even the moths trembled.

Sometimes I could distinguish Papa's wine-soaked groans spilling into the yard after he'd taken another gulp from his amphora and dipped once more into the leather purse secured to his belt. Sometimes he'd gnaw at the flesh around the tip of his thumb and spit out the pieces, his mind elsewhere while his tongue flicked like a snake's. And sometimes I could spot a crescent of his face swollen with that same passion to win that I'd seen in Binyamin the day he strangled young Titus. But as Papa's self-confidence degenerated into desperation, he became a crazed caricature of his former self, someone I hardly recognized.

Why was Papa gambling with a bunch of thugs? And more to the point, why was he gambling at all? Was this his way of recovering his solvency? Or was this the way he'd lost it? Was he holding onto the scrolls as a last resort to settle his gambling debts?

As if he'd heard my questions, he got up from the table and staggered out the door not five paces from my crouch. But rather than answer me, he lifted the skirt of his tunic to relieve himself. The steam of his offerings and the sound of his grunts rose above his squat while the ground beneath me swayed.

"Hey, those Jew dogs are no better than the rest of us, huh Glaucus?" From the sound of this grotesque, I guessed he was the thug sitting next to the Enforcer. He spoke in a drunken, guttural voice and had a face so long and eyes so far apart that I named him the Horse.

The whoops of wild laughter he triggered settled into consensual snickers.

I'd seen and heard enough. As soon as Papa ducked inside and resumed his place at the table, I figured a way to get out from behind the garbage heap and back to the lane without the bearers seeing me. I'd cross the rear yards until I happened upon another alley that led back to the lane, and by keeping the lighthouse in my sight, I'd find my way through the maze of lanes around the saloon and guide myself due south toward the Canopic Way.

Confident of my plan but acting too quickly, I tripped on the tail of a scruffy mutt while crossing into the next yard. I pacified its whine with Phoebe's sesame cakes, but it was too late. The bearers had awakened from their thin stupor. Armed with their lanterns, they combed the yard, shafts of their light grazing me as I scurried behind the next building.

Only to confront a fierce black hound.

Hackles up.

Snapping, snarling, growling.

Challenging me.

Its fiendish eyes ablaze.

Its stiletto teeth threatening.

Foam dripping from its flews.

Poised to spring.

I drew back, dropping my lantern, my own jaw agape.

Whipping out the carving knife, gripping its handle, raising the blade.

Just before it lunged.

Its stiff whiskers brushing my jaw.

Its steamy breath coating my neck.

A clammy chill against my blistering skin.

The blade rushing downward, slicing the air, slashing the fur, then the throat, defying the bone.

The head diving forward.

The trunk and limbs crumpling at my feet.

Spurting a geyser of blood.

And a spray of excrement.

Splashed with its sticky splatter, unclenching my fingers, dropping the knife but recovering the lantern, I bolted. Charging helter-skelter down one lane, up another, drenched in fear, a stitch in my side, my heart pounding, my lungs billowing, my chest heaving, my airways wheezing, I paused only when I'd reached the Canopic Way. While I was catching my breath, I heard the first wave of peddlers and wondered what lie I could tell Papa if his bearers had recognized me crossing into the yard next to the saloon.

PHOEBE WAS EXACTLY where she said she'd be, watching for me from that same sitting room window. She must have seen the arbor's canopy sway as I tripped through its tunnels because she'd materialized in a rectangle of light by the time I reached the bed of chrysanthemums. Upon opening the window, she leaned out with her index finger pressed to her lips. I flashed a beam of light from the lantern to acknowledge her warning, whereupon she tossed out the end of my bed sheet, now coiled and strung with knots. She'd moved the sofa under the window and tied the other end of the sheet around one of its legs so, when I shinnied up the few feet to the windowsill and she hoisted me in, I landed on its cushions.

What would I ever do without my Phoebe? Gratitude filled

my chest like warm honey.

"Miriam, what's happened to you? You're smeared with filth." The corners of Phoebe's lips were trembling.

I had to search a few moments for my tongue. "Oh, that's just from the hound I killed."

I explained all that had happened, except, of course, for Papa's bodily functions. I couldn't bear to tell her that. But I did tell her about the darkness, the narrow twisting lanes, the wine shop, the saloon, the ruffians, the gambling, Papa's losses, the mutt and the hound, the sesame cakes, and the carving knife.

I remember Phoebe's preparing me for bed, bathing me and mixing for me a sleeping draft of chamomile tea fortified with opium before unrolling the pallet so she could sleep beside my couch. Still, I had a chaotic dream about that monstrous hound, that same black Saluki, but now twice the size, towering over me. Not just the one but a pack of them, seven swift hunting hounds bounding in for the kill.

Panting feverishly.

Their legs trembling.

Their yellow eyes feral.

Their shadows leaping toward me.

Their frenzied howls enclosing me.

Their frothy muzzles pointing at my throat.

Their fangs bared.

Their luminous tongues licking the air.

Drooling sparks of foam-streaked saliva.

First nipping at my feet. Then gnawing at my legs, my blood spewing, their flews dripping a slaughterous red, their ferocity mounting.

I must have screamed when their teeth tore off my limbs, because the next thing I knew Phoebe was wrenching me from the tentacles of the nightmare. Kneeling at my side, she cradled me in her arms, subduing me with her coos and wiping the perspiration from my brow.

We both knew the meaning of that dream.

"If you go out like that again, Miriam, you'll surely be killed."

Chapter 18

Late Tuesday Morning

PHOEBE BURST INTO my *cubiculum*. "Miriam, your father's been asking for you. He wants to see you right away."

The alarm in her voice wrenched me out of a blessed unconsciousness. I would have given anything but the scrolls to plunge back into that sweet oblivion, but Phoebe had already awakened the memories the sleeping draft had anesthetized—the wine shop, Papa's gambling in the saloon, the hound from Hades, and the stink of its blood and excrement.

"What do you suppose he wants?" she asked, her features frozen with apprehension.

I was too thick with sleep to answer. Instead, I rolled over and slipped down into the warm envelop I'd made of my sheets.

Phoebe yanked on my bedding, reached over my shoulder, and thrust the polished bronze mirror from my washstand in front of my face. "Do you want him see you like this, Miriam?" Her imperious fuss reminded me of Iphigenia when she'd have to get Binyamin ready for school.

She helped me change from my rumpled *capitium*, the light chemise I wear for sleeping, into a long yellow sleeveless tunic made of polished linen dyed with saffron. Then she twisted my hair into a loose braid and slipped a pair of sandals on my feet, crisscrossing the ribbons around my legs and tying them in a bow just below each knee.

"There," she said, turning me around. "I can't say you look great with those half-moons under your eyes, but you're presentable. Now go to your father."

Why was he summoning me? Surely he couldn't have found

out that I'd followed him. My shadowy memory of last night triggered a spasm through my bowels, while the dread of yet another reprimand kept distracting me from counting the steps as I made my way to his study.

And then, standing at the threshold, I saw it. Through the open doors and before his unyielding gaze. On the otherwise-bare surface of his polished desktop. The silver-handled carving knife.

Compressing my lips and swallowing hard against the gelatinous reflux that surged up my gorge and coated my tongue with bile, I took a seat before his desk, moving slowly while I rummaged through my repertoire of lies for some semblance of an explanation.

A shaft of light from the peristyle backlit his upper body and projected a thickened silhouette of him across the desk. He'd been drumming his fingers on the arms of his chair, but when he saw me, he leaned forward and rested his hairy forearms on the desk.

His gaze poked me like a sharp stick.

"How do you suppose I got this, young lady?" He spit out the words in a voice choking with fury.

With his thumb and index finger, the other fingers splayed, he lifted the knife by the merest corner of its handle. Then, extending his thick arm, he thrust the tapered edge in my face, the filth still smeared along its blade.

Splinters clogged my throat. I could only shrug, my hands at my sides, my palms turned up.

"Well, I'll tell you how. My bearers gave it to me. They said someone dropped it. How do you suppose your mother's favorite carving knife ended up in the *Bruchium* Quarter last night?"

Another spasm ripped through my bowels. This one turned my insides watery.

"They told me about a shadowy figure who'd been following them as far back as the Canopic Way, some slender man, a slave, they said, judging from his *lacerna*. But he disappeared before they reached the inn. Only when the whine of an animal alerted them did the beam of their lanterns catch a piece of him as he darted behind an adjacent building. And then they dared not desert the chair to follow him. But Orestes got curious and decided to find out what the man could have been after. He found the fresh corpse of a Saluki and this knife, which he brought back to prove his pluck and present for a reward. He could hardly have imagined I'd recognize the knife as coming from my own household.

"Surely if it had been Binyamin, he'd have chosen a more appropriate weapon, if in fact he'd have thought he needed to bring one at all. So either you or Aunt Hannah must have been taking in the air in the *Bruchium* Quarter last night."

At that moment, the room shrank around me, and I hated him for his sarcasm.

"I wasn't following the bearers, Papa, I was following you. You went to a saloon, not to an inn. And not an ordinary saloon, mind you, but a backroom gambling den with the kind of ruffians you said Binyamin would consort with on a voyage to Rome."

The pitch of my voice clotted with rage, each word cutting through his arrogance like the carving knife had slashed through that fiendish hound's throat. And my tone reverberated with a cruel satisfaction, even pride, for standing up to his bullying, for unleashing my own brand of intimidation, for turning the tables to give him a dose of his own medicine.

So I continued.

"And there was one ruffian in particular who caught my eye. When he wasn't swilling his Negrito, he was relieving himself in the yard. I hardly recognized you, Papa. What's become of you?"

I crossed my arms, preparing for another gust of sarcasm.

Instead his expression morphed from denial to indignation and finally to remorse and shame as he collapsed into a private agony.

At first his mouth moved, but the words died in his throat. So, pushing back his chair, he levered himself up on shaky legs, wiped his sweat-drenched palms across the belly of his tunic, and dragged his chair to my side of the desk while I slid mine over.

As he turned toward me, the weepy gray light from the peristyle illuminated one side of his face.

"Miriam, my dear Miriam, it was bad enough having you interrogate me as if I were a common criminal, as if I'd absconded with the family jewels, but I cannot have you loitering in blighted alleys in the dead of night. That was reckless of you. You are the light of my life and the future of our family. You must not do that again."

My rage began to leak away.

"I too have been reckless," he said. "With the delay in announcing your marriage date, my relationship with Amram has soured. You know I am a proud man, Miriam, that I live by my word. So I cannot be at ease with him anymore. I cannot face him. I have broken the pledge he and I made when you were a toddler and Noah was a skinny lad, the very pledge, reaffirmed over the years, that became the cornerstone of our partnership."

His back rounded now, his head bowed, his arms crossed in his lap, he continued softly, with a catch of emotion in his voice. His lips barely moved except for a self-pitying sigh.

"So, I've been trying to raise the capital to buy Amram out of our shared investments. At first the goal seemed attainable, but Alexandria has prospered despite the burdensome taxes and outbreaks of civil strife. So our assets have appreciated. And with Noah's adding new mortgages to our holdings all the time, I saw my goal, paradoxically, becoming harder and harder to achieve.

"That's when I turned to gambling, first on the chariot races—only the long shots, mind you—and then on dominoes and twelve-card draw in my club, but as my losses outstripped my winnings, the stakes got too high for me. So I had to find lower-ante games.

"You're right, Miriam. I hardly recognize myself. The only way I could consort with those ruffians was to get good and drunk, to drown my shame and wallow in my indignity."

Anger and pity, sorrow and disgust, horror and compassion

each took a turn vying for my emotions. But when I took his hand in mine and pressed it to my lips, I saw a disarming candor and surprising gratitude illuminate his eyes for the first time.

All this man has ever wanted for me is a secure future with a loving family. Is he to be condemned for that? Why can't I just explain to him that I don't want to get married? That I'm not the reincarnation of Yocheved. That I don't want children. That I don't even like Noah anymore, at least not when I'm with him. That I want to study alchemy and learn about keeping the body and spirit of both humans and metals healthy. That all I want is to recover the scrolls before they find their way onto the black market. Before Jews are crucified, scourged, drawn and quartered, immolated, and butchered. Before our businesses are razed. Before there's another pogrom.

On the other hand, why can't I just marry Noah and solve all our problems? Why can't I set the date and heal the breach and restore my father's honor and ease Amram's grief and have a houseful of children? Why can't I do what every other maiden in our quarter would love to do, to marry into an adoring, honorable, and prosperous family? Instead, I vacillate. I'm unable to resolve the dilemma, even though I think of little else except the betrothal and now, of course, the scrolls. And with the end of the week bearing down on me—I have only a little more than three days left—I'm no closer to solving that problem either.

So I also confessed.

"Papa, I too am living with a shame that will haunt me for the rest of my life. I borrowed priceless scrolls, and despite my promise, I could not return them. Someone took them from my cubby in the library, probably during *Shabbat* but certainly between Friday afternoon and Sunday morning. Someone who knew what they were and where I kept them. Someone who had the opportunity to take them. Why someone would do that to me, I do not know. But I need to know, Papa. Was it you, for whatever reason? To tarnish my standing with the League of Alchemists, to spur my marriage to Noah, or to sell them so you could sever the partnership and restore our solvency? Please,

Papa, for my sanity. Please, for the inviolable bond between us. Please tell me. Did you take the scrolls?"

"No, Miriam. I did not. On my word of honor, I did not take your scrolls. Nor do I know who did."

So it was Binyamin.

Chapter 19

Tuesday Afternoon

I DIDN'T HAVE to look far for Binyamin. His expletives were billowing out of the library like smoke from the lighthouse. When I peeked in from the courtyard, he was sitting at the now-scarred cherry wood table, the restrained northern light backlighting his face. He was wearing a green sleeveless, knee-length tunic of fine Indian cotton girded at the waist with a leather belt, which, like his sandals, was studded with multicolored Alexandrine glass beads. One hand was folded under his chin to support his frown, while the other tapped a steady rhythm with his stylus against a wax tablet. Binyamin was never still.

The lingering scent of ash feathered my nostrils as I entered, the maids having mopped the floor after sweeping up the shards of pottery and splinters of glass. They'd replaced the lamp and restored the arrangement of the furniture but left to Phoebe and me the task of re-shelving the thousands upon thousands of scrolls. The room smelled empty of not just the shattered artifacts but the very souls of my mother and father, who, in better times, must have celebrated the acquisition of each vase and figurine.

As soon as Binyamin spotted me, he dropped his stylus and curved his arm around the tablet. Too late. I'd already seen what he'd been working on, a list of provisions for a voyage to Rome.

"Are you really going?" I asked.

"Maybe someday." He let his answer hover. But then, tunneling his lips, inhaling deeply, and leaning back in his chair, he added with a sigh, "Yeah, Sis. I'm leaving soon, but that's a secret. I'm not looking forward to another row with Papa."

Yes, I thought, he'll leave as soon as he sells the scrolls. He'll get many times the amount of money he'd need to go in style, and knowing Binyamin, that's exactly how he'd go.

My foot hooked a leg of the chair across from him. When I dragged it out and sat down, Binyamin leaned forward.

"So, how are you getting ready?" Was my attempt to pump him as obvious to him as it was to me?

"I'll finalize the arrangements tonight."

I took that to mean he hadn't sold the scrolls yet.

"That soon?" Despite my effort to sound calm by speaking slowly and distinctly, my voice was thin with tension, and my head whipped back as if he'd kicked me in the face. An alarm buzzed through me at the thought of his fighting in the arena, but the hope of recovering the scrolls tingled down my spine. I had only three days left.

"Who knows?" he asked with a shrug and turned-out palms. And then, as an afterthought and with a snicker, he added, "Are you afraid I'll miss your wedding? Because you've really done a number on Noah. If there's such a thing as being lovesick, he's terminal."

Binyamin would mock Noah whenever he could because Noah had become the son to Papa he could never be. I can still remember the time—Binyamin and I couldn't have been more than six—when I realized that Papa favored Noah over his own son.

Papa and Amram had hired two litters to take Noah, Binyamin, and me to the Pharos Lighthouse. Noah's sisters were too young to go. I remember our litter with its fringed canopy and polished bronze fittings carrying Papa, Binyamin, and me behind lace curtains, the warm odor of the padded leather interior intensifying the intimacy.

Cruising high above the crowds that clotted the Canopic Way and the Street of the Soma, we glided through the din of commerce, the clang of foundries, and the clamor of warehouses before crossing onto the *Heptastadion*. There we whizzed past a party of Syrian tourists, a fuel convoy, and a band of pilgrims headed for the Temple of Isis. The bearers slowed only to thread us through a platoon of soldiers. Taking a break from the heat and the weight of their enameled cuirasses, they lay spilled across the roadway. Binyamin sat forward to wave first to them and then to the thick-necked sentries guarding the small fort at the end of the causeway, while I sat back to watch the current slap against the hulls of the thousand and one ships and listen to the rigging smack against their masts.

The bearers deposited us on the shore path just beyond the causeway so we could walk the rest of the way. Aside from the lighthouse, I wanted to see the abandoned village Hector had told me about. Many of its houses had been ravaged by fire during one of the battles Julius Caesar fought with Cleopatra, but the entire village had to be abandoned when Caesar's forces demolished the aqueduct that carried water along the *Heptastadion* to the island. Anyway, we didn't go, because Papa said that Amram shouldn't have to look at the relics of death and devastation even if the village was destroyed almost a century ago.

Bending into the wind, we followed the shore path's curve along the Great Harbor walking single file for about a mile, first east, then north, and finally east again to the lighthouse. Salt-laden gusts thrashing the weeds that lined our path snapped the hem of my tunic, whipped my face, and filled my nostrils with the odor of raw seaweed. At times a spray from the breakers would catch me by surprise and coat me with its lacy foam, but I would just pretend I was a sea captain caught in a squall, fighting the deafening gusts, the pelting rain, and the heaving waves.

By the time I managed to steer my imaginary ship through the squall, the others had reached the Aswan granite pillars that frame the courtyard of the lighthouse and were craning their necks in wonder at the marble and bronze Tritons that adorn the triple-tiered, marble-faced tower. The first tier is square, the second, octagonal—I remember both their observation decks were jammed with tourists—and the third, cylindrical. But my attention fixed above the third tier, to the lantern and the polished mirrors that spread its light and then to its cupola, capped by a weathervane of Poseidon poised with his trident to either calm the seas or stir a storm.

I asked Noah to read me Posidippus's epigram, which is inscribed on the tower. I can only remember some parts, the ones about the tower appearing "to cleave the sky from countless stadia away" and a sailor seeing "a great fire blazing from its summit," but Noah didn't get to finish anyway because Binyamin, impatient to get inside, kept pounding on Papa's thighs with his fists.

To reach the entrance, we had to hike up a steep, two-story ramp supported by sixteen graduated arches. Papa's armpits looked like they'd melted by the time the two scarlet-caped Roman sentries admitted us—from the bottom of the ramp, they'd looked like a pair of statues—and permitted us to start the eighteen-story climb toward the first observation deck.

As we circled through the odors of mice and brine, our jug-eared, pimple-faced guide directed us up the broad interior ramp that spirals around the core of the lighthouse. The cones of sunlight from the western windows spilled their amber glow onto the damp stone floor before casting our furry shadows onto the eastern wall. As we passed the hundreds of immense rooms, our guide explained that the ones pierced by windows are for housing the mechanics and attendants. The others, he said, are for storing the stacks of resinous wood and the amphorae of oil and bales of reeds that fuel the lantern's fire when the wood is in short supply.

A file of mules three abreast passed us hauling carts of wood from the storage rooms to the top of the second tier. There slaves would unload the carts and carry the fuel to the lantern. When Papa said that for a fee, the mules would also carry tourists, Noah complained of being tired. I remember Papa caressing his bristly hair and taking his hand, but when Binyamin asked for his other hand, Papa called him a big baby. Amram took Binyamin's hand, but it wasn't the same. And hasn't been since.

My mind was finding its way back from the lighthouse to

Binyamin's scorn when he added by way of an apology, "I just meant that Noah is crazy about you."

In a fit of pique, I folded my arms across my chest. "It's still not funny, Binyamin." But then I felt my face relax and my lips soften. "The truth is, I'm distraught over the betrothal. I don't want to marry, and even if I did, I wouldn't want to marry Noah. As devoted, as rich, as shrewd, and as sympathetic as he is, he's become repulsive to me. But I don't seem to have a choice. Papa's heart is set on the marriage, the sooner the better."

"Yeah, that's Papa all right, so good at directing everyone else's life. He acts as if he knows what's best for us, but he's really just engineering what's best for himself."

He turned a thickening gaze toward the window.

"Remember when we were kids how I used to sneak off to the games to see the gladiators?"

I didn't answer. I could tell he had more to say.

When his eyes found mine, he continued.

"other tiI loved the entire spectacle, beginning with the fanfare that starts the parade into the hippodrome. But my favorite part was when the gladiators, accompanied by jugglers, clowns, and acrobats, would circle the arena in detachments according to their various schools. My own heart would beat in time with the trumpets, flutes, and drums that accompanied them.

"Those gladiators! They'd look like gods as the early morning light defined every muscle in their well-oiled bodies. And the young women mooning over them! Intoxicated by their own erotic fantasies, they'd throw the gladiators kisses and beckon them with lewd gestures."

Fascination was warming the chill in Binyamin's eyes.

"Before the bouts they'd sacrifice a bull in homage to the emperor, but not an ordinary bull, Sis. This one would have its horns gilded for the occasion and its flanks draped in garlands. Between the blare of the trumpets, I'd hear the priests intone their blessings as they hovered to subdue the poor beast. Then, amid the smoke of incense, knives would flash until the animal cowered to its knees and its blood stained the sand. After that, the smell of fresh meat burning on the altar would signal to the impatient fans that the spectacle was about to begin.

"Next, either wild beasts would fight each other, or better yet, a lone gladiator would face a single beast. That's when you'd see the dignity and discipline of Rome, Sis. I'll never forget one gladiator, slight, naked but for a loincloth and a film of sweat, armed with only a thin sword and a frozen, tight-lipped grin. His opponent, a broad-backed Numidian lion, trotted into the arena from its underground cage. Whether stunned by the glare or bewildered by the noise, it swept the sand with its tail, apparently too dazed to fight. But when the gladiator scooped up a handful of sand and flung it in its face, the lion snapped. Snarling with rage, its ears flattened, it hurled itself through the air, its sunlit claws aglow like amber, its tufted tail a streak across the arena. In an isosceles stance, the gladiator plunged his sword into the heart of the beast, but not before it stood on its hind legs and clawed the flesh off his jaw. Gushing his own blood, the gladiator nevertheless raised his sword to salute the prefect and bow to the spectators. And then, leaving a trail of crimson to mark his path across the arena, he disappeared behind an iron grille."

The image of the triumphant gladiator danced in Binyamin's eyes.

"Before Augustus they'd follow the sacrifice with the *andabates*. That was when a dozen or more gladiators wearing helmets without eyeholes blindly brandish their swords while the *mastigophori*—they're in the arena to goad the fighters—prod them one toward the other with long-handled pitchforks. That must have been hilarious.

"But the best part would come next, the bouts featuring a pair of gladiators. We'd thrill to at least ten of them, like the ones between a *retiarius* and a *secutor*, who train to fight each other. The *retiarius* is the only one who fights without a helmet, no leg armor, only a loin cloth, some strapping around his left arm, and a bronze shoulder guard extending to his elbow. Unlike the *secutor*, he has no sword, only a trident and a wide-mesh, circular throwing net. Sis, you should see how resolute a *retiarius* is, even in the face of death."

Binyamin was saying more now than I'd ever heard him say before.

"The *secutor*'s helmet both protects him from and makes him vulnerable to the *retiarius*'s net. Enclosing his entire head, the helmet is smooth and with a rounded top so the net can slide off easily, but its tiny eyeholes narrow his field of vision. So the *secutor* has to get close to the *retiarius*, well within the reach of the net. Now that's what I call a match!

"And you should see what happens when it looks like a gladiator's been killed in the arena. A 'Mercury' or 'Charon' presses a red-hot iron to his body, and if he moves, the faker's throat is cut then and there before he's dragged off to the *spoliarium*. You know what that is, right, Sis? That's the pit where the bodies of the slain beasts and gladiators are dumped until the mass burial."

I continued to hear his words. I suppose I could have even repeated them, but I no longer had the forbearance to make sense of them, let alone challenge them with an objection that Papa hadn't already preached a million times. So I just let him talk, listening only when he mentioned Papa again.

"Papa knew how much I loved the games, but would he ever take me? Would he ever enroll me in a *collegium iuvenum* so I could study the martial arts? Oh, no. That wouldn't be appropriate for a son of his. I had to become an ephebe. That's Papa. So, if he says you're going to marry Noah, then knowing you, Sis, that's exactly what you're going to do."

Splotches of sweat now stained the front of his tunic where it clung to his chest. Shaking his head and pressing his eyelids shut with his fingertips, he was silent so long I wondered whether he'd continue. When he did, the sun had already inched past him to illuminate his stylus, and his voice was thick with guilt.

"You know, I understand Papa. I really do. I did a heinous thing, ripping open our mother's belly like that, killing her as surely as if I'd cut her throat in the arena. But you forgave me, you who'd also lost a mother and had to grow up in the shadow of that pokerfaced idol of his. He never has. To him, I'm a killing machine, like one of Hero's gadgets. Tighten the valve here, adjust the spring there, and you can count on Binyamin to kill anything."

His eyes lost their focus for a while, as if he were recollecting a long forgotten nightmare, but then their focus returned.

"So, yes, Sis, one way or another, I'm going away, and I'm going soon. I just have to work out the details. Why shouldn't I do what I was meant to do and, in the process, become a celebrity? I'm not his son, and I don't want anything from him, not his name, his house, his money, nothing, not now, not ever."

I knew I'd live to regret it, if I lived at all, but I couldn't help myself. Right then and there, dream or no dream, I resolved to follow Binyamin to find out how he was going to finance his voyage. And if someone was buying the scrolls, I vowed to recover and return them to Judah before it was too late.

Chapter 20

Tuesday Night

"BY THIS TIME tomorrow, Phoebe, I'll have the scrolls."

"Really?" she asked, tipping her head back, clapping her dumpling-like hands, her girlish face wreathed in a smile that outshined the candlelight in my sitting room.

"Binyamin has them. He took them to finance his voyage to Rome. I think he plans to sell them to a broker tonight since you heard nothing about them yesterday in the agora."

"Binyamin would do such a thing to you? I can hardly believe it."

"I know, Phoebe. I'm sure he still doesn't grasp the significance of the scrolls to me and every other Jew in the Empire. He's just so desperate to get to Capua."

"So how will you recover them? Are we going to sneak into his suite and, under cover of darkness, steal them back?" Phoebe rubbed her palms together with conspiratorial glee while her voice melted into a soft giggle.

"No, Phoebe. I'm going to follow Binyamin tonight to see who the broker is. Besides, Binyamin wouldn't have the scrolls on his person or, for that matter, in this house. By now, he'd have secured them in the Public Records Office. But by tonight, I'll have proof that he has them, and when I explain why I need them, I'm sure he'll give me the token to claim them."

"So why not just ask for the scrolls now?"

"Because I need proof. Soon he'll be leaving, and I may never see him again. The last thing I'd want him to remember is that I accused him of something without proof, even though I understand only too well his need to get away from Papa.

"Besides, tonight won't be like last night. He'll be meeting a businessman, not a bunch of thugs."

"Miriam, you must not go."

"You know I have to."

"At least take the bodyguard. Your father already knows you're intent on recovering the scrolls."

"But he mustn't know that Binyamin's departure is imminent, and besides, one person can slip through a darkened street more easily than two."

Phoebe drew her eyebrows together and shook her head as if to ward off the prospect of my going. Then she sat down, slumped forward, and her shoulders began to shake.

"Miriam, I know you'll be killed tonight. How could the scrolls be worth your life?"

"They are my life, Phoebe, and you can help me save them. Just keep watch and signal me with a knock on my door as soon as Binyamin leaves."

She let out an extravagant sigh to tell me that yes, she'd do it, but no, she didn't like it one bit.

I should have listened to her Cassandra-like prophecy.

GAZING THROUGH one of my sitting room windows waiting for Phoebe's signal, I watched the moon slide behind the cypress trees and the navy blue sky surrender the last of its color to a star-speckled blackness. Sure that Binyamin would be meeting the broker in a respectable neighborhood and realizing that once I heard them negotiating, I'd no longer need to hide, I wore my himation rather than a disguise over my tunic.

But instead of wrapping the himation around my body, I veiled my face. I centered the thick, woolen rectangle across my nose and mouth, wrapped the tails around the crown of my head, fastened them under my chin with my mother's fibula, and let the ends drape behind my back. Then, as soon as I heard the knock, I grabbed the portable lantern, jumped from the window, and like last night, scrabbled through the arbor, using the fire of the lighthouse to orient me toward the street.

Savoring the clarity of the night air despite its chill, I followed the shaft of light from Binyamin's lantern and the soft tread of his boots in a silence that was otherwise absolute save for the treetops sighing in the sea breeze. Passing the occasional gauzy yellow square that was a candle-lit window—perhaps the home of a colicky baby or a worried couple—we soon found ourselves on the torch-lit Canopic Way. Surely we were nearing his destination.

But no. Binyamin was not slowing his pace. On the contrary, his strides had lengthened so much that I could hear my breathing labor in concert with the trees' obbligato, and I could feel a gloss of perspiration coat my chest despite the sharpening chill. Having long since crossed the Street of the Soma and turned south, the lighthouse was now well behind me. The buildings speeding past me were no longer faced with marble and stone, not even with plaster painted to resemble stone, but with mud bricks scarred with graffiti.

A sinister smell seeping out of the darkness alerted me that we were near the canal. That and our position farther west than I was last night meant only one thing: We were inside the malignant *Rhakotis* Quarter.

Binyamin's pace slowed.

What in the Name of G-d was he doing here?

He looked around, perhaps for the broker, although why they'd meet in this canyon of squalid buildings I couldn't fathom. A moment later someone shouted from a marble-topped counter opening onto the street. Upon closer inspection, I saw the counter was the front of a cookshop tucked between a dilapidated tenement—its shutters bashed in, its door weathered to silver—and an empty warehouse.

A primordial giant as menacing as a Cyclops stepped outside to fill the beam of Binyamin's lantern. Inasmuch as he wore an *exomis*, a short, left-sleeved, laborer's tunic that bares the right side of the wearer's chest, I fixed on the stump that had been his right arm. But when Binyamin swept the giant's face with his lantern, I was fascinated more by the purple wart perched on the end of his nose and the ichor trickling from his swollen eyes. Try as I might, I couldn't tear my gaze from that weepy discharge. When he called to Binyamin again, this time by name and with a roar that ripped the stillness, I recognized him as the illustrious ex-gladiator Sergius.

Stories about Sergius still surface amid the swirl of gossip in and about the agora. That he'd been seen here or there, at the games or at the theater. That a *retiarius* had once stabbed him near his left ear with a trident, a blow that, notwithstanding his helmet, had cost him his hearing in that ear and dented his skull. That Eppia had given up her several hundred slaves, her villa in Rome, and her seaside estate at Antium after falling hopelessly in love with him. And that her husband, the senator, was still searching for them. Don't tell me they've been hiding these last three years in some flea-infested, piss-soaked apartment in the *Rhakotis* Quarter!

So Sergius was going to broker the sale of the scrolls. He escorted Binyamin into the cookshop and waved him toward one of two chairs around a table just behind the counter. Once Binyamin was seated, Sergius poured him a tankard of henket and offered him hunks of a steamy cardamom bread and skewers of roast lamb that released a whisper of mint.

Well within their aromatic range, I longed for some of Phoebe's sesame cakes.

I scooted low and in close, wrapping myself in the tails of my himation, crouching behind the charcoal-burning furnace recessed into the cookshop's marble-topped counter, grateful for the steady fire that kept the kettle sputtering and the sharpening chill at bay. Only occasionally did I dare lift my shoulders to peek inside.

The counter, open to the street, crossed the front of the cookshop from its doorway to its side wall, a distance of about seven feet. Then it turned into the shop at a right angle to offer several more feet of counter space along the side wall. The rest of the wall was fitted with graduated marble shelves for storing the shop's glassware, cutlery, and crockery. Several large paintings, all of men in a latrine, covered the back wall, each with a descriptive title, none leaving anything to the imagination.

The portly counterman, probably the owner, must have just finished washing the tableware in the basin under the counter, because the sink gurgled as he rubbed his hands across the long, once-white, grease-spattered apron that dipped below his paunch. Then he lifted its skirt to wipe the sweat that had accumulated on the single shaggy eyebrow that spanned the bridge of his nose, and with a corner of that skirt, he traced the notches and grooves inside each oversized ear. After that, he began to refill the clay wine jars distributed at intervals along the counter and embedded in the masonry beneath them.

At first I heard only Sergius and Binyamin's wolfish intake of food and drink, their utensils grating against the tin plates, their greedy gulps and smacking lips punctuated by grunts of satisfaction. But after a while, Sergius pushed his chair back from the table, and they began to converse. I could understand Sergius despite the harsh vowels of Vulgar Latin that peppered his Greek, because his tone was strident, common enough among the hearing-impaired, and facing the front of the shop, his words rolled over the counter and into the street.

"Yes, I still have a contact there: Rufinus, the *lanista*. He manages the *ludus* in Capua along with buying, selling, and hiring out his own gladiators. Anyway, he'll decide how you'll be trained and assign you to a coach, an ex-gladiator who specializes in that weaponry. With a face like yours, he'll probably assign you to train as a *retiarius*, since they fight without a helmet."

Another glimpse told me that Binyamin had squared his shoulders.

"As a volunteer rather than a slave, criminal, or prisoner of war, you'll sign a contract that specifies your period of obligation, your earnings, which will be no more than twenty-five percent of your prize money, and how often you'll fight—probably once a month. At the point of signing and for the duration of the contract, you'll be the property of the *lanista* and the school. You'll live locked in a windowless cell about three yards by four yards. You'll share the cell with another gladiator and spend most of your time within the solid brick walls of the school. You'll train in a small, elliptical arena guarded by men wielding clubs and whips, and you'll take your meals with the other gladiators. You'll eat a high-energy diet of beans, dried fruit, and barley, the barley to coat your arteries with fat. That's to reduce bleeding. You might travel to distant cities, but you'll always be brought back to Capua."

Binyamin interrupted with questions, but Sergius dominated the conversation, with, so far, no mention of the scrolls.

"Your exit visa will cost you about four drachmas (the value of eighty pounds of barley) if you register as an unskilled laborer."

Now at least they were talking about money, but still nothing about the scrolls. Sergius went through all the incidental arrangements and costs, beginning with boarding Binyamin and storing his provisions at The Pegasus—the waterfront inn and warehouse likely to be closest to his pier—until the ship's herald announces her departure. I missed most of the other details. I was so distracted by the tributaries of henket dribbling from the sides of his mouth and washing into that nasty humor leaking from his eyes, but he ended with Binyamin's overland transportation from the Roman port of Ostia to the school in Capua.

He explained that there's no way to predict a ship's departure date. First, the winds have to be favorable. Then the pre-sail sacrifice of a bull has to go well. Next, the time of the month has to be auspicious. No Roman skipper would depart at the end of a month. And the omens must be propitious. A sneeze on the gangplank, a wreckage on the shore, or a croaking crow or magpie perched on the rigging would delay any departure. So would someone's uttering a foreboding word or dreaming of turbid waters or goats, especially black ones. Similarly, dreams of wild boars or bulls, owls or other night birds portend a storm, pirate attack, or worse yet, a shipwreck. Consequently Binyamin might have to wait at the inn for weeks.

"And don't forget," Sergius continued, "If a storm approaches, be sure to cut your nails or your hair and throw the clippings overboard. That might avert a disaster. But if you're caught in the storm, tie any jewelry you have to your body so anyone finding your corpse would have the money for your funeral."

That's when Binyamin dropped his skewer of roast lamb and looked up.

I had trouble assimilating all the details—my legs had cramped in the crouch and I'd started to shiver—but I gathered that a ship from Alexandria to Rome has to take a roundabout course to counter the Etesians. She has to sail along the southern coast of Asia Minor to Crete, Malta, and Sicily rather than head directly for Rome. In other words, under the best of circumstances, the voyage would take at least two months.

Sergius offered more details, and then, after a string of mumbles from Binyamin and my mounting doubts about learning anything about the scrolls, he mentioned financing.

"So, yes, I'll accept your mother's jewelry as collateral for my stake, which will cover the entire cost of your trip from here to Capua. As soon as you sign this promissory note, based on your talent as an athlete and in exchange for five percent of your prize money and half of your signing fee, I'll advance you the cost of your exit visa and book deck passage for you on the next grain ship to Rome."

Binyamin exhaled a long breath.

"Deck passage means that you, like most of the passengers, will sleep on the deck. The ship will supply only water and a hearth in the galley for you to use during certain hours after the crew has finished. I'll supply a tent to shelter you on deck, along with a mattress and bedding. I'll order your shipboard provisions for eating, bathing, even defecating, and I'll arrange for everything to be transported from the inn's warehouse and loaded onto your ship. And I'll have your supplies replenished in Crete and again in Malta. Once you get to Rome, I'll advance you the funds to hire a mule and carriage to take you to Capua, outfit yourself for the journey, and stay at inns along the way."

As if he'd recited the list a million times, he was ticking off each point by folding a finger of his left hand into his palm.

"Depending on the weather, you'll stop in Aricia, Bovillae, Tres Tabernae, and Forum Appii. You'll have your choice of inns at any of these places. Don't worry; they'll be easy to identify. Even if you arrive late at night, you'll spot them. They all keep a lamp burning above their door. In the daytime, you'll recognize them by the erotic scenes painted on their façades. Wait till you see the ones on The Camel in Aricia and The Sword in Tres Tabernae. I guarantee you'll get a kick out of those!"

Knowing Binyamin, I'd guarantee it too.

Sergius's face had split into a wide smile, but then, a businessman again, he wiped his mouth and continued.

"Anyway, you'll get food, wine, and lodging in a room with a cot, chamber pot, and candle holder. Of course, you'll have to share the bed with as many fellow travelers as can cram in, but you'll have an opportunity to change your mule and carriage, relax in the public baths, and hire a prostitute. Just watch out for the *copa*. She's the woman who runs the inn. She'll be no more scrupulous than the captain of the ship or the owner of the livery stable, even though she's a woman. Every one of them is notorious for adulterating the wine, and that's just the beginning. Believe me.

"Oh, yeah. I almost forgot the most important thing. I'll give you a letter of introduction to Rufinus."

So why weren't they discussing the scrolls? Why was Binyamin offering his share of our mother's jewelry for collateral and promising Sergius a cut of both his prize money and signing fee? What other use could he be planning for the scrolls? And then a thought came to me like a final, shameful, crushing blow: that I'd been lying to myself all along. Neither Papa nor Binyamin had taken the scrolls, and I was never going to recover them. But before I'd let that despair immobilize me, I was going to find my way out of this pestilential underbelly of the city.

Chapter 21

Late Tuesday Night

I BLUNDERED HALF mad through the streets and haunted alleys, sometimes darting and dashing, other times tucking myself into the entrance of a tenement, edging my way, swiveling my head, listening for any creature that was about, suppressing my every shriek, swallowing my every whimper, pinning my every hope of survival on my position relative to the lighthouse. Only when its flames split the darkness above my left shoulder would I know that I'd escaped the claustrophobic *Rhakotis* Quarter. Only then would I be beyond the reach of the thieves and murderers who lurk there preying on the nameless and dumping their corpses into the canal to soak, bloat, float, and then putrefy in the next day's baking sun. Otherwise, I felt only a hunger in the pit of my stomach that was the will to survive.

The fading glow of my lantern did little to disperse the shrill parade of macabre creatures that flitted across the screen of my imagination. Instead, they bred in the formless, flickering shadows that the lantern struggled to cast. The face of every tumbling tenement, the stench of every dank alley, and the scratch of every whirling piece of trash whispered veiled threats in my ears. At the same time, the dread of never recovering the scrolls coated the back of my throat with bile.

I neared an alley between the shell of an old slaughterhouse—no amount of sand or sawdust could blanket its stench—and an abandoned brewery, its only remaining door propped open with refuse, its yard choked with weeds and unidentifiable debris. Panic seized me. Something malevolent was seeping out of that alley. I couldn't tell whether it was a sound or a smell, but some sentient life form was hovering in the squalor of that alley, on edge, poised for action.

I stopped.

Snuffed out the lantern.

Held my breath.

Footsteps? More than one pair?

I tiptoed to the mouth of the alley and bent forward.

Holding my breath.

Craning my neck.

Listening.

Was I hearing only the cold? Perhaps a breaker battering the rocks, fanning its spray into the sky. Or the whine of the wind whipping the treetops or rustling the underbrush. Or the echo of clattering hooves. Or the growl of a feral dog. Perhaps only the chatter of locusts, the yawn of a soldier, the squawk of a gull, or the groan of the Earth itself.

Was I smelling only the darkness? Perhaps the odor of the bricks, the tang of the sea, or the putrefaction of a carcass. Perhaps the vapor of my own stale sweat, the piss of a cat, the hair of an old dog, or the droppings of a sick mule. Perhaps the breath of a stable yard, the reek of rotting wood, the fetor of dying weeds, a derelict's curdling vomit, a spill of posca, or an accumulation of the night's panic and neglect. Or perhaps something more, like the odor of damp wool and the stink of male tension.

Was that the crunch of a boot on gravel? The swoosh of a *lacerna*? The beat of a heart quicker than my own?

The soft hairs on the nape of my neck warned me.

My fear blossomed.

I heard a voice like the hiss of an angry snake.

"He's spotted us."

Four panther eyes converged on me, as hard and glassy as flint.

Ditching their sacks.

Grabbing and flinging my lantern.

Pungent cloaks spinning.

Chilly belt buckles attacking me.

"By Zeus, it's a woman! Kill her."

A punch to my belly.

My guts somersaulting.

Loops of pain wrapping around my abdomen, rippling outward, shooting down my legs.

I pummeled the air and, spinning around, caught a left hook that split my temple and shrieked in my ear.

The ground rushed toward me.

Their grunts spiraled downward.

A stinking cloak muffled my cries.

A solid uppercut to the side of my head.

After that, a right hook and a bubbling cut.

A new galaxy of stars.

The blur of a kick.

Another.

Then I lost count.

I saw my mother in a nimbus of light.

"Good. She's dead. Help me wrap her corpse in her himation. We'll dump her in the canal and come back later for the loot."

"Her fibula! She's a Roman citizen. Gods and goddesses of Mount Olympus, what in Hades is she doing here? There'll be soldiers, a search, an investigation. They'll trace the loot. They'll arrest us, crucify us"—

"Run! Never mind the"—

My bones screaming like the blare of a siren, I separated from the filaments of pain and drifted into a private darkness.

Chapter 22

Wednesday Afternoon into the Night

LODGED SOMEWHERE in that intricate world between life and death, I drifted between the reality of a ringing, catastrophic pain in my left ear and a black, silk-lined delirium in which words floated about but had no meaning. Impressions of the events that had brought me here flicked before me in a sequence of ghastly images washed of color. But somewhere at the edge of that vision, through the slit that was the puff pastry of my left eye, I saw Phoebe.

"Am I in a tomb, Phoebe?" I could taste a sour whistling as the words came out, and whenever I moved, I felt the thieves' fists pummeling my belly.

"You're here, in your *cubiculum*, Miriam, and you're safe. Close your eyes and rest."

Lolling my head back, I eased into the pillow and curled onto my right side. I must have slipped back into a semi-consciousness where my memories met my imagination, where I was not yet ready to tackle the pain and even less ready to face the sliver of time left to recover the scrolls, let alone set my wedding date. Yet I was aware of the fading daylight arcing across my lids and my body taking an inventory of its working parts. And through the veil of my stupor, I sensed Phoebe at one with the shadows, cleansing my cuts, massaging my muscles, rubbing verbena into my temples and hands, feeding me barley broth fortified with the foul-tasting ash of beef bones, and treating me with a poultice of mossy herbs to combat the swelling around my eye. Finally, by the cool touch of night, I'd spiraled out of the daze with a need to know what had happened.

"Tell me again where I am, Phoebe, and how I got here." I tried to sit up and open my eyes, but all I saw were sparks against a swirling blackness. So, clutching my belly, I curled back onto my side and closed my eyes.

"You're right here with me, Miriam, safe and sound in your *cubiculum*. It's Wednesday night. Nestor brought you here. He'd finished his stint in our market and was making his late afternoon deliveries to the restaurants, cookshops, and *kapeleia* across the city when he found you in the *Rhakotis* Quarter in an alley beside an old slaughterhouse. At first he thought you were just another pile of rubbish, but when the sun caught the gold in your fibula and threw a disk of light against the pavement, he stopped, and upon recognizing you, dumped his remaining produce in the street, lifted you into his cart, and brought you home. He can't imagine what you were doing there. Needless to say, I said nothing, but he's concerned about you."

"I thought Binyamin would be meeting a broker around here. Otherwise I'd never have worn the fibula." My words dribbled out on a lacy strand of spittle.

"It saved your life, Miriam. Your mother was watching over you and praying to Isis that you'd be rescued. So Isis sent Nestor to prevent your nightmare from coming true. I remember your mother always wore the fibula. She told me your father gave it to her as a wedding present, as a symbol of not only his love for her and her rank as a Roman citizen but of their family's future. His grandmother and mother had it before her, and when he gave it to your mother, he told her that someday it would belong to their daughter. I remember Iphigenia putting it away each night and bringing it to your mother every morning. Nestor's finding you proves that your mother wants you to study alchemy."

"But the fibula didn't save my mother's life, Phoebe, and the truth is I wish it hadn't saved mine. I don't have the scrolls, and I have no idea where they are and how I can get them. I know only that Binyamin took them. But I can't accuse him because I have no proof. So there goes my career as an alchemist, over before it began. I might just as well marry Noah, who doesn't care about my honor or my shame, my ambitions or my fiascos."

"I know your mother wants you to live. She valued life, and I say that not just because she saved mine. You're too young to know how tenderly she took care of me, but I remember. Before I would go to sleep, she'd bathe me and clothe me in one of the embroidered linen nightdresses she'd been saving for a daughter. But she took care of strangers too. On Friday afternoons, she and Iphigenia would deliver scores of meals to the poor, wonderful meals, the same food the cook prepared for your parents' *Shabbat* guests. And your mother delivered them to not just the Jewish Quarter but the *Bruchium* and *Rhakotis* Quarters as well, to soup kitchens throughout the city. She said it was her holy obligation, but she did it anonymously so no one could feel beholden to her."

My mother continues to be a living presence for Phoebe.

"You too are generous, Miriam. You honor your father with your mother's tradition of hospitality, and you protect your brother by helping him with his lessons and shielding him from the brunt of your father's temper.

"Iphigenia told me that when your mother realized she was dying, she made your father vow that no matter what happened to her, he would see to it that Binyamin and you—despite your being a girl—would have the best possible education. So your father purchased a slave to escort your brother to a school that would prepare him to enter the Gymnasium as an ephebe, and he purchased Hector to tutor you at home. I can still hear Hector bragging to your father about you, that you were a *disciplina bona* (a good disciple), that you worked hard to learn, and that you knew Latin so well that you could masquerade as the emperor's wife.

"So I know your mother wanted you and Binyamin to have a life of your own choosing. You don't have to marry Noah. You can manage this household and your father's investments and do anything else you want. You don't need Noah for that."

Her compassion bubbled through me.

"You too, Phoebe, should have the life you want. Surely my mother would have wanted that too. As soon as I'm up and around, we can apply for you to become a free resident of Alexandria."

"Miriam, I've told you before. You are my family and my life. I want to go wherever you go. And now it's time for you to get some rest. I'll bring you a sleeping draft, and in the morning, we'll see what the day brings."

Chapter 23

Thursday Morning

OTHER THAN A pulpy black eye, a bump on the side of my head, and a few eggplant bruises from my hard landing and where the thieves had kicked me, I didn't look so bad. Phoebe had brought me an early breakfast of another bowl of barley broth and a dose of hellebore for the pain, so I felt no worse than yesterday, ready to face the day—in this case to speak with Binyamin, proof or no proof. He was bound to ask me about my wounds, and given his imminent departure and the fast-approaching deadline for my returning the scrolls—only two days until *Shabbat* and then I'd have to see Judah on Sunday—I convinced myself to be direct with him. So, after slipping a short, sleeveless tunic over my *capitium*, I knocked on his door.

Entering his suite, I saw him poised on one knee before his sleeping couch, the sole of his front foot pressing into the floor to balance his weight. He was leaning over the tousled bed linen, a few pieces of our mother's jewelry laid out alongside two sheets of papyrus, a pen case, his seal, and a silk-lined drawstring pouch. He must have been making an inventory for Sergius and a copy for himself, recording a description of each piece before slipping it into one of the many pockets of the pouch. I wondered with a sorrow that filled my throat whether our mother's Alexandrian pearls were among the pieces he was assigning to Sergius. When finished, he'd draw the strings closed, melt a stick of wax across the flap that folds over the mouth of the pouch, impress the wax with his seal, and tuck the pouch inside his belt.

The morning sun poured through his open windows, its lemony light spilling across the mosaic floor, catching the gleam of his perspiration, spinning his skin into gold. My eyes surveyed his sparse, austere furnishings: a sleeping couch flanked at its head by a wicker chair and at its foot by a cedar wardrobe, its doors open, his remaining tunics, sandals, and boots in a jumble at the bottom, some spilling out. The other furnishings were a freestanding brass candlestick and his athletic equipment, namely a set of barbells and bench, an exercise mat, and his discus. Otherwise, only a ripe tang filled the room, his own heady scent mingling with the odors of stale bedding, candle wax, last night's cheap wine, and above all, sadness.

He'd been up for hours, judging by the film on the food that remained on his breakfast tray, the length of the inventory, and the plumpness of the pouch, but the barber had yet to bathe and shave him. Barefoot and wearing only a bleached cotton robe, he'd set aside in one corner of the room a pair of boots, an embroidered linen tunic with a belt and matching sandals, his chlamys, which is a sporty traveling cape shorter than a himation, and an Iberian leather travel bag crammed with sundries.

Seeing the bag was a more stunning blow than all of last night's kicks and punches combined. The rest of reality dissolved around me as if I were viewing it through a tunnel, this single leather bag packed with the essentials, perhaps a memento, and all the sorrows of his childhood, its antagonisms, disappointments, losses, and rejections. My fist flew to my chest as if it could plug the puncture in my heart and blunt the realization that today he would leave this house forever to kill or be killed for the cheap entertainment of a mob.

Binyamin turned to look up at me, interrupting the whirl of childhood images and emotions I thought I'd blotted out years ago. Then, squinting against the light, he waved me toward the chair.

"Whoa! What's happened to you, Sis?"

"I wanted to speak to you about that."

Edging back and settling onto the seat of the chair, I angled toward him, my arms folded across my thighs.

"I was out the other night, doing something foolish I know, spying on you in the *Rhakotis* Quarter. I was trying to recover the scrolls taken from my cubby between Friday afternoon and Sunday morning. Thinking you might have taken them to finance your trip and were about to sell them, I'd hoped to interrupt the sale and convince you to return them to me. On my way home from the cookshop, I met up with some thugs. As for the rest of my story, the purple welts speak for themselves."

He hunkered down before me, his head thrust forward like a turtle's. Narrowing his eyes, he looked me over, his forefinger under my chin, turning my head from side to side. Then, brushing aside the pouch and sheets of papyrus, he sat across from me at the head of the couch.

"My G-d, Sis, you look terrible, but I have to hand it to you. You've got nerve." And then, tipping his head back and chuckling, he added with a nod, "You are definitely my twin."

"I'm sorry to have blamed you for taking them. I first thought Papa had done it, but when he convinced me he hadn't, I had to conclude it was you."

"You can't be serious."

"Who else could have known where the scrolls were? Who else could have been alone in the library, and who else could have hoped to benefit from taking them?"

"But how could a few scrolls finance a voyage? What do they contain, the secrets to eternal life?"

"They're more dangerous than that. They contain experimental recipes, albeit incomplete and purposely obscure to confound the uninitiated. But more important, the information in the recipes could incite another pogrom."

"By Zeus, what on earth are you mixed up in, Sis?"

I wasn't going to open up that topic so I asked him how he happened to get Sergius to finance his trip.

When he paused and took a deep breath, I knew I was going to hear a long story.

"I used to see Sergius at the games, where everyone would make a fuss over him, but I didn't get to meet him until I became an ephebe. He would come to the Gymnasium's *palaistra* to watch us wrestle. I noticed he began to pay particular attention to me, coming to all my events, even the pentathlon in the stadium. After each of my competitions, we would talk, sometimes in an exercise room or the baths, sometimes in the garden.

"He told me about his life as a gladiator, how by volunteering, his debts had been forgiven and he came to be accepted as a member of the school's *familia gladiatoria*. He even earned the title of best combatant, *primus palus*, and was ultimately awarded the *rudis*, a wooden sword symbolizing his permanent discharge. But mostly he talked about the thrill of living on the edge and becoming a popular hero.

"You see, Sis, volunteers are treated better than the prisoners and slaves condemned to the arena. Yes, we too have to swear allegiance to the gods of the Underworld; be tattooed on our face, legs, and hands as property of the school; and submit to the rules of the barracks, but as valuable property, we're fed well and treated by physicians trained right here in Alexandria. And the duration of our service is limited by contract."

I would have liked to remind him that he'd still be a slave, a warning my father surely had reiterated countless times, but his face beamed with so much pride that I held my tongue. Anyway, it would have been useless.

"So, over the last few months, with Sergius's encouragement, my fantasy has become a reality. And he told me that after I retire, I could become a trainer, manager, or even the owner of a *ludus* in the provinces. He himself earns commissions from managers all over the Empire by sending them athletic young men likely to withstand the rigors of training and attract a following. But he earns most of his income by investing in prospective gladiators like me, financing their trip to a *ludus* and collecting a share of their signing fee and purses."

I listened raptly, shifting my position only to ease the jab of a wicker spine against one of my bruises.

"We reached an understanding more than a week ago and

met as planned at the cookshop so we could review the conditions of our agreement and I could sign the promissory note.

"Late this afternoon at the pier, he'll give me a letter of introduction to the *lanista* in Capua and another to the Bank of Gabinius in Rome, where, through our branch in Alexandria, he's established one account to fund my journey to Capua and another to collect his share of my signing fee and prize monies. In return, I'll give him our mother's jewelry to hold as collateral, accept delivery at the warehouse of the provisions he's ordered, wait at the inn for the herald to announce the ship's departure, and direct his porters to load my provisions onto the ship."

Given his mastery of these particulars, I wondered whether Binyamin might have made a better business partner for Papa than Noah.

"Sergius explained that I might have to wait weeks at the inn, but he has an arrangement with the *copa* to accommodate me indefinitely, everything included, even prostitutes."

In one rhythmic sequence, Binyamin flicked a smile and waggled his head in disbelief at his good fortune.

"Once in Rome, I'll wait for the next tournament with Rufinus's gladiators, sign a contract with him there, and travel to Capua with the troupe, or I'll hire my own mule and carriage and take my time getting there.

"So today I'll leave this house for good, and except for you and Aunt Hannah, I'll be glad to leave everyone else."

"Will you at least say good-bye to Papa? He really does love you and, in his own way, has wanted the best for you."

"No, Sis. I couldn't bear another row with him. Besides, since *Shabbat*, we're like two ghosts. We occupy the same space, but we're invisible to each other. So I think it's better if I just leave."

"But please," I said as I lifted myself out of the chair to grasp his hands. "At least let me accompany you to the pier. I'll hire a curtained litter to wait for us on our side street so no one will witness your leaving or stare at my bruises, and together we can have one last spin around the city in style."

He shrugged as if he had no choice and then managed a stiff smile.

So I ordered a litter for that afternoon. I only wished I could have ordered the scrolls to appear as easily. If Papa didn't take them and Binyamin didn't take them, then who did? And how and why did they do it? With only one more day to find out, the last flutter of hope was dying in my breast.

Chapter 24

Thursday Afternoon into Early Evening

SHADING OUR EYES like cave dwellers, we tiptoed into the sharp afternoon light, swiveling our heads in unison like a dancing duo to make sure no one was about. Then we rounded the corner to view our waiting litter, its fittings like molten gold under the baking sun, the polished ebony bodies of its eight Nubian bearers resplendent in their starched white tunics threaded with gold. Dizzy with the prospect of gliding through the streets high above the ox dung, I could pretend that we'd be riding on the wings of Mercury. That we'd be sealed in a compartment, invulnerable to the realities of time and space. And that we'd be on a celebratory outing rather than playing out the last scene of our shared history.

Folding ourselves into the compartment, we settled facing one another on overstuffed cushions scented with rosewater, Binyamin's bag at his side. Spikes of sunlight tamed by the lace curtains warmed my face and intensified the excitement in Binyamin's eyes before spilling into the gold-threaded interior. Then the bearers lifted the litter to sweep us southward through our quarter to the Canopic Way, westward to the Museum, northward on the Street of the Soma through the agora to the Caesareum, and finally along the harbor to Binyamin's pier in the *Eunostos*.

"I really appreciate this send-off, Sis. I know you've been worried about me. But remember, I'm not studious like you. I could never spend the rest of my life bent over a ledger like Papa and Noah. So I figure this is my best option. I could have enrolled in the *ludus* here, but I wouldn't have the same opportunities for training and competition that I'll have in Capua. Besides, I need to make the break for Papa's sake as well as my own. Can you imagine his reaction if I were training right here in Alexandria?"

Some change in his expression, perhaps the slight parting of his lips or the lifting of his eyebrows, told me that he was taking the moment to enjoy that fantasy.

"Binny, Binny, Binny, of course I've been worried about you." I didn't let on how worried, beginning with the voyage itself, not only the risk of a storm but the certainty of shipboard scoundrels waiting like vipers to feed on him. I only hoped he couldn't hear the apprehension in my voice.

"You're a part of me," I said, "the better part considering your grit, even as a child daring to confront Papa regardless of the consequences, something I'm still not able to do. And yes, I believe you could have a future in the arena. I just hope you're not doing this to atone for our mother's death. Papa may blame you, but her destiny was determined long before we were born."

"No, Sis, I really do love the games. You know I don't respect many things, but I do admire the Roman virtues gladiators represent: their discipline and dignity, their physical form and fearlessness, and their will to win. And Sergius says I have the gift.

"I admit I've borne Papa's blame, but you've kowtowed to him. You've let him plot your future even though it means marrying someone you find repulsive. By the way, I find Noah repulsive too."

"My reasons for marrying Noah are complex, but mostly I think it would be best for the family"—

"You mean best for Papa. Look, I know you're interested in someone else. Don't blush, Sis. The whole quarter's been gossiping about it. You are, after all, our Aphrodite. They see you in the agora—and I don't mean on just the calends—without Papa's bodyguard and when you could have sent Phoebe."

I gawked at him, biting into my lower lip before dropping my chin and tracing anxious circles on my himation with my index finger. But then I remembered the gaggle of matrons in the agora, their multiple chins shaking, their lips pinched in disgust as they pelted me with impudent stares.

"Oh, Binny. No wonder Papa's been insisting I set the date."

"There you go making excuses for him again. You don't have to marry Noah just because Papa says so. Life is short. Take it from me: Pursue pleasure. That's the only lesson I remember from school, that one class in philosophy, that pleasure is the supreme good, and bodily pleasures are better than mental pleasures. To me, being a gladiator means pursuing those pleasures both in and out of the arena."

The scar on his left cheek wiggled in synchrony with the rhythm of his voice.

"You know, Sis, I've never been afraid, certainly not of Papa. To me, his punishments were inane. Why should I care whether he grounded me? I'd just jump out my window and go wherever I wanted anyway, to the Gymnasium or Zenon's cookshop, to hang out, gamble a little, or lure his voluptuous daughter into the pantry, where she'd flaunt her vulgarity and I'd relieve my lust."

Binyamin made a lewd gesture with his hands.

"In a sense, I had more freedom when I was grounded, because I didn't have to explain where I was going, and you were ready to swear that I'd spent the evening studying with you. I only wished he'd have grounded me from school."

This time when his lips parted, they curled into a full smile.

"Still, Binny, I'd have this recurrent nightmare that he'd caught me in the lie and turned me into a bronze statue that looked like Medusa after Athena had punished her."

He threw out a whoop of laughter, but when he saw I was serious, his guffaw froze in the air, his face puckered, and he shook his head as if to say I was a hopeless ninny.

"Listen, Sis, you'd feel guilty when you were in the kitchen and the cook broke a plate."

Peeking through the curtains, watching the scenery slide by, I noticed we'd already turned onto the Way, its otherwise deserted concourse speckled with a few heat-drugged vendors hawking parasols and honey-sweetened water inside sharp-edged slivers of shade. Our bearers, their feet barely brushing the pavement, loped through the *Bruchium* Quarter, turning its colonnades and fountains, temples and monuments, sphinxes and statues into a radiant blur. Soon we'd reach the Museum with hardly a chance to glimpse at Eratosthenes's astrolabe under the portico of its soaring central hall. Or squint at the shimmering marble dome of the Museum's circular dining hall. Or crane our necks to gaze at the top of the observatory. Or watch the scholars saunter along the tree-lined walks to the Great Library. Or peer into the surrounding park, its arcades, botanical gardens, ornamental pools, and statue of the Muses.

Casting about for any anecdote to forestall the doomsday silence that was threatening to blanket our litter like a toxic gas, I told Binyamin about the time Hector took me to the Great Library. Nowadays, anyone literate can access its manuscripts, but we had a special invitation because Hector knew the director. They'd studied together years ago, long before the burden of a dying brother's *laographia* forced Hector to sell his freedom to Papa.

Hector had to chide me for gasping when I entered the vaulted reading room, the Library's largest and airiest hall. The beams of sunlight streaming through its arched clerestory windows were exploding into countless beads of light. Some splashed onto the fluted stone pillars and the bearded busts of the Library's greatest scholars who peered out at us from every niche. Others glinted off the marble walls and the rows of multicolored Alexandrine lamps. At the same time, secondary beams polished the long, narrow mahogany tables and warmed the finial-topped, leather-cushioned armchairs.

The readers were scattered among the tables. Several sat back brooding over their cache of scrolls while their curling sheets of papyrus, inkwell, and tray of sharpened pens lay idly about. Others were hunched over their papyri, scratching notes furiously. I lingered to watch them as if I could absorb their erudition by breathing in the hall's scents of leather and tranquility. One scholar with a tonsure of orange frizz and unkempt whiskers was leaning back with his arms folded across his chest, waggling his head and jiggling his leg in bafflement. Another, a white-haired Arabian with a prognathous jaw, stared at the ceiling's covings while scratching his head and squinting into the light. A frail, hollow-chested Carthaginian bowed his head and bit his lower lip when his hulking colleague rebuked him for his dry, concussive cough. And a red-faced Iberian with a crooked nose and a harelip wielded a torn scroll in an insistent arc to summon a tiptoeing slave to bring him a replacement.

As self-conscious as I felt when Hector chided me for gasping, I buried my face in my hands when he had to do it again, this time in a less-than-patient baritone "for clopping like a horse on cobblestones." (The patter of his sandals on the dark-veined, polished marble squares made hardly an echo.) But the image of a horse in this very hall prompted me to burst into a fit of giggles like the side splitters I'd have with Phoebe. As if my lack of control weren't mortifying enough, when it launched Hector's wayward iris into a clockwise spin, I succumbed to yet another, more hysterical fit, this one punctuated by snorts, croaks, and hiccoughs and culminating in a puddle on the floor.

Never mind that I'd come to see the double-door meeting rooms, lecture halls, recital theaters, and refectories. That I longed to feel the weight of the silver door levers and smell their metallic residue on my hands. Never mind that I'd set my heart on seeing the director's office. His collection of rare scrolls is rumored to fill every cubby on every wall from the dado to the carved wooden ceiling. Never mind that I'd also dreamed of gazing at that ceiling's stunning design, an optical illusion inlaid with red, green, yellow, and rarest of all blue jasper. And never mind that Hector had promised to show me the Museum's vivisection laboratories.

An unbidden gag escaped from Hector's throat, one he hastily converted into a dry cough. The blood that had drained out of his now stony white face must have rushed into mine because I could feel my throat throbbing, my color reddening, and a wash of sticky sweat pearling across my forehead. Instead of continuing our tour, Hector tugged at my elbow and hustled me into one of the many chambers that flank the hall. Each must store hundreds if not thousands of scrolls, but I noticed only the chamber's ancient dust and the acrid odor of its greasy tallow wicks. With my eyes already burning and my nose beginning to sting, I dreaded yet another fit, this time of sloppy sneezes, wet and explosive.

Slaves on ladders were shelving and fetching scrolls from immense storage cabinets while others were hauling armloads and basketfuls to waiting readers. In one corner, three bearded scholars sat huddled over a table stacked with layers of unrolled manuscripts. Hector explained that they were comparing different Homeric texts to ascertain the canonical version, which, as a source of income for the Library, scribes would copy for wealthy bibliophiles around the world.

I was diverting Binyamin with this story of my outing with Hector when, distracted by a flock of twittering sand martins on wing to the beach, I peeked through the curtains again to see that we'd already passed through the agora. Spotting the sprawling emerald lawns of the Caesareum ahead, the vast cityscape that dominates the Great Harbor, and hearing the sea thunder and hiss against the rocks, I realized with a bile-swirling jolt that our jaunt was almost over, that the present was sliding toward the future all too quickly.

Soon we'd be entering the grounds of the Caesareum. Perhaps for the last time Binyamin would gaze upon its gilded statues of nymphs and goddesses; its galleries, banquet halls, and libraries; its porticoes, promenades, and reflecting pools; its terraced gardens sloping to the sea; its leafy groves and thickets; its sculpted fountains and topiary; its courtyards redolent of roses, the beds backed by jasmine hedges and the walls lined with espaliered fruit trees.

Next he'd gaze upon the temple itself, its entrance heralded by two great obelisks known as Cleopatra's Needles, its façade burnished to a pale amber in the late afternoon light. Wounded by his own sword, Mark Antony died here in the arms of his Cleopatra, and she, having failed to beguile Octavian, provoked the bite of an asp to die here eleven days later in the arms of her handmaidens.

Instead of viewing the sights, Binyamin had lowered his chin. With his eyebrows contracted, he was pressing his palms against his cheeks, his fingertips against his lids. But a moment later, he was Binyamin again. Having won his struggle for that Roman self-control, he lifted his chin and pasted a thin smile on his otherwise impassive face. Afraid to test the durability of that smile, I looked away to pluck at the folds of my himation before unfastening our mother's fibula.

"Here, Binny, I want you to take this for protection."

At first, he leaned back, squinting and cocking his head. But when he saw the fibula in my hand, he raised his shoulders and straightened up. Tossing some cushions out of the way and holding onto the side of the litter for balance, I inched toward him on my knees.

For a moment, while I was pinning the fibula to the right shoulder of his chlamys, I felt a prick behind my eyes and thought our tears might mingle. But no. Only his shallow, rapid breaths and the heat of his body betrayed his stress.

Then, thrusting his arm through the undulating curtain to signal the bearers to stop, he said in a flat voice, "I have to go now, Sis." Before his words could melt into the warm breeze, the bearers had lowered us to the curb. Grabbing his bag and bolting through the curtain, Binyamin began a run toward his pier while I stayed to listen to the rhythmic jingle of the clasps on his travel bag and watch his figure become a minified silhouette in the fading daylight and then disappear.

Chapter 25

Thursday Evening

"HOLD STILL, MIRIAM."

"But Phoebe, it stinks."

"You want to walk around with that bruise on your face forever? You look like you're wearing a rotten plum." Phoebe could make me smile even when she was bossy.

We were in my sitting room, the sea breeze rustling the crowns of the cypress trees while the candelabra threw amber stripes across the mosaic floor tiles and into my *cubiculum*. I was sitting at one end of the sofa, on the edge of the cushion, my knees crossed, one leg twisted around the other like a vine. Phoebe was standing over me fussing with the poultice, refolding the warm, mustard-filled cloth to secure it around my head with a strip of linen. I was relaxing in the pleasure of her sweet breath against my cheek when, with a frisson of excitement, I noticed a rolled-up sheet of papyrus on my writing desk.

"Phoebe, what's that?"

"You know that twisted little man, the hunchback I see begging in our plaza when I go to buy produce from Nestor? He slipped me this letter when I was serving your aunt lunch in the courtyard. He'd been waiting by the curb, and when he spotted me, he called out and handed it to me through the thicket. I'm lucky I didn't scratch my arm on the thistle when I poked my hand through the fence."

"Did you say you scratched your arm?"

"No, I said I was lucky. But he scratched his."

"Did he call you by name?"

"Yes." After a thoughtful pause, she added, "I wonder why he didn't just come to the front door."

And I wondered why the sheet of papyrus had been sealed without the sender's mark. But I'd know soon enough. I managed to break the seal despite my trembling fingers and read the scrawled message aloud in a voice stressed to a high pitch:

"miss bat isaac, stop tryin to recover
the scrolls r sumtin bad will happn."

Then I heard a thud.
Phoebe had toppled over.
Her face now bloodless.
Her eyes rolled back.
Her jaws locked.
Her limbs rigid.
Her chest drenched in sweat.
Her body vibrating in short, rapid, rhythmic waves.
"Phoebe!"
No response.
"G-d Almighty, what's happened to my Phoebe!"
I moved the desk out of the way, turned her on her side, and wedged a pillow under her head.

Her spasms beat an eerie tattoo against the tiles for a minute or two. Then I heard a gurgle and a gasp for breath. Her twitching had subsided, her jaw had slackened, and her eyelids were fluttering. She looked around in wonder as if adjusting to the details as they trickled back to her.

"You're okay, Phoebe. Everything's going to be all right." I cooed these assurances with only the pretense of confidence. Then I kneeled and, straddling her body as I faced her, threaded my arms under hers, locked my hands behind her back, and slowly raised her to a sitting position to ease her breathing.

I waited, listening to the silence until she was ready to speak. At last she released a few words in the stream of a sigh.

"What happened to me? I started to feel numb, and after that I don't remember anything."

No one had to tell me what had precipitated Phoebe's seizure. But as alarmed as I was by her convulsions, I was comforted by the letter itself. I realized the thief was feeling threatened and the scrolls were still recoverable, which meant they hadn't been sold and hadn't left Alexandria. Second, I realized the thief knew us well enough to anticipate Phoebe's routine and call her by name.

"How are you feeling now, Phoebe?"

"I'm all right, just sleepy. But I'm afraid. I don't want you trying to recover the scrolls anymore, but I know you will. That's the way you are."

"A terrible wrong has been done not only to me but to the League, something that could hurt all the Jews in Alexandria, even the whole Empire, and I'm the only one who can right that wrong."

Aside from the thief, of course.

Poor Phoebe. I sounded as egotistical as Papa. So I softened my tone. "I'm also afraid, Phoebe, but whoever the thief is, he's more frightened than we are, and knowing he's afraid bolsters my resolve."

All the while I must have been trying to imagine the thief's modus operandi because as soon as I said the word "resolve," it hit me. Phoebe hadn't scratched her arm, but the hunchback had.

I struck my forehead with the palm of my hand. Here I'd been flailing about for days trying to discover who the thief was, and if it wasn't Papa or Binyamin, how he'd managed to steal the scrolls out from under our very noses. And Phoebe had just given me the answer. My thoughts crystallized now on what had been unthinkable before. With rekindled hope, I bolted out of the room to search for the key witness, Aunt Hannah.

Chapter 26

Late Thursday Evening

"IS THAT YOU, Miriam?"

I hardly recognized the timbre of Papa's voice. Its raspy edge had been worn smooth.

Crossing the atrium, I peeked into his study and saw a shadow of his former self hunched over his desk, one elbow perched on the desktop, his slackened jaw leaning into the palm of that hand. Sadness lived in every crease of his face.

"I was looking for Aunt Hannah, but one of the maids told me she'd already gone to bed."

"So come in and sit down. Please." He waved me toward my usual chair and then studied my face.

"You're bruised, Miriam."

"Oh, never mind that, Papa. I'll tell you about that later."

I had no intentions of doing so.

"Let's sit in the peristyle, Papa. I like the smell of the greenery in the evening." In truth, I couldn't bear to sit dwarfed before his massive desk anymore.

As our sandals clicked against the marble tiles, he called for a maid to light a tallow lamp and bring us some cinnamon cakes and mint tea, and then we took seats across from each other on the teak benches that curve around the stone table. Aside from the hanging baskets of ferns and the ribbons of ivy coiling around and festooning across the pillars, planters of peonies projected their stout shadows across the tiles. Their foliage bowed and swayed while the perfume from their deep pink blossoms mingled with a sea breeze that had dismissed the heat of the day but had yet to usher in the chill of the night.

After the maid served us and Papa excused her, he took a deep breath, paused, and then reported with a stoic face and a lifeless voice, "Binyamin's gone. Late this afternoon one of the maids preparing to clean his room found his door ajar, his clothes strewn about, and his travel bag missing."

Papa looked at his tea. He curled his huge hands around the glass but didn't lift it. "I drove him away," he said, shaking his head to ward off the incomprehensible.

The rising moon cast a blue light on his black hair while the flickering lamp alternated between illuminating and obscuring the furrows across his forehead. He twirled his glass around with the tips of his fingers before he spoke again.

"I remember when we went to the Serapeum for Binyamin's induction ceremony, how gratified I was that he'd have the advantages of an ephebe. He'd begin his day in the lecture halls studying all the subjects I loved: grammar, literature, rhetoric, music, logic, astronomy, and geometry. I knew he wasn't scholarly like you, but I thought the competition would motivate him to study.

"After his studies, he could thread his way along the Gymnasium's shady colonnades through a campus so immense and grand that Augustus himself used it as a public place to address the city. Depending on the sports of the day, Binyamin might go to either the covered track to run or the *palaistra* to wrestle or box; on another day, to either the field to throw the discus and javelin or the *korykos* to punch the bag.

"After that he might enjoy the sauna, the hot and cold pools, or a massage at the Roman-style baths. Or he could amble over to the water gardens, where he'd relax and socialize while cooling himself in its fountains. Still later, he could saunter under the covered gallery past the wrestling arena to the theater. There, before ending the day at an evening banquet, he might watch the latest play, fascinated like the rest of the audience by Hero's special effects: the thunder and lightning, the 'gods' flying through the air, and the rotating scenic backdrops. Or he might listen to a politician charm the crowd. How gratified I was that I'd be fulfilling my promise to your mother to give him the best possible education."

I also let the memory of that day wash over me. I'd been to the Serapeum only twice, the first time as a young girl to tour with Aunt Hannah, Iphigenia, and Phoebe its cool labyrinth of subterranean crypts and corridors. We passed cavernous chambers of bare stone breathing out their ancient must, some for stocking the scented wood for the temple's fires and flambeaux, others for storing its sacrificial instruments, ceremonial utensils, and sacerdotal robes. Mostly though I remember my nose tingling from the scents of frankincense, myrrh, and nard in the laboratories where they manufacture the cones of incense.

We were barred from some of the rooms: the chapels for ascetic worship and contemplation, the dungeon for those guilty of a sacrilege against the god, the living quarters for the monks, the refectories for the functionaries and servants, the vaults for the temple's most precious treasures, the stalls and stables for its sacrificial animals, and the well-stocked arsenal to defend the precinct and its enormous wealth. Still, we were able to pick our way through the meeting halls and the kitchens with their soot-streaked walls, enormous hearths, bakeries, pantries, and wine cellars, each chamber a hive of activity dappled by the sputtering light of smoky, oil-fed torches and ripe with the smell of sweat on unwashed bodies.

When we were escorted out of the cellars and I'd cleared some of the dust from my throat, I noticed short messages, scores of them, scrawled on the stone walls where the daylight had penetrated. Most of the graffiti were in Greek, many in verse, all dated, some even mentioning the author, his profession, and homeland. I wanted to scribble my own verse until Iphigenia warned me that I could be thrown into the dungeon for a desecration like that. As soon as she said that, I thought of the scores of manacled souls rumored to be incarcerated inside its moldy walls.

But Papa was ruminating on the second time I'd been to the Serapeum, when I'd gone to meet him there two years ago. He'd hired a chariot to carry him up the carriage road, but I'd set out earlier and arrived long before he did. My legs first running, then aching, I climbed the steep, one-hundred-step spiraling marble staircase, which was flanked by rows of sphinxes from the base of the acropolis to the vast quadrangle of white stone at its summit. Having reached the highest point in Alexandria, I was rewarded with a merry breeze and a panorama of the miniaturized city while I rested on a stone bench until the pricking in my lungs eased.

Lake Mareotis and the countryside beyond unrolled before me toward the south. As I raised my hands to shade my brow, my eyes were drawn to the bustle about the lake. Brown-skinned women shouldering baskets of laundry to and fro along the sandy paths, others either bowed over their garments, kneading them while the water lapped at their feet and the wind snatched their chatter, or crouching to spread them out on the rocks to bleach and dry. Barefoot children frolicking along its marshy fringes. Ibises perched on their stilt-like legs, probing the mud with their long, down-curving bills. Gangly boys up to their knees in the stagnant water, cutting down reeds on fleshy stems and collecting them in baskets strapped to their backs. Houseboats squatting in the papyrus beds, their occupants fishing off the deck. Punters propelling cargo in their flat-bottomed boats with a push of their pole against the lake bottom. And ferries zigzagging across the tea-colored water from town to town, slicing through beds of Egyptian-blue water lilies.

When I'd finished counting all the ferries, I raised my eyes to the fertile countryside beyond the lake. Meandering lanes dotted with outbuildings too numerous to count cut the landscape into orchards of silver-barked olive trees, arbors of twisted grapevines, and golden fields of barley, castor beans, and emmer wheat.

Tendrils of damp hair fanned out from the back of my neck when I turned to view the sea stretching to the northern horizon, its surface whisked by a breeze that billowed a thousand sails. My gaze dropped to locate the intersection of the Street of the Soma and the Canopic Way, and from there my finger traced the route to our house and up the side street to Noah's.

Now, sitting across from Papa, I stifled a yawn. Silently studying the tabletop's swirling patterns instead of listening to his bleating account of that day, a story I'd already heard so many times, I remembered leaving the lookout point with its vistas still imprinted on my memory. I crossed the chariot road, and feeling each marble tread bake through the soles of my leather sandals, I mounted the expansive stairway to the six-columned Doric façade of the Serapeum's gatehouse. Once inside, dwarfed by its coffered ceiling of carved marble blocks, I cut my way around the throng of visitors, filed through the ornamental bronze gate that was guarded by a cloudy-eyed, muttering old priest, and ventured into the sacred precinct's dazzling light.

Hector had taught me about the cult of Serapis. So I imagined Hector with me, together our strolling about the gardens and lecture halls. Our meandering through the Daughter Library's collection of hundreds of thousands of manuscripts. Our circling the cult's stadium, where thousands celebrate the power of their god with annual games. Our catching glimpses through the colonnaded porticoes of the priests' long, narrow residence halls. Our studying the shafts of the temple's four Aswan granite columns, wrought to tell the story of their god's mythical incarnation. And our marveling at the immense doors to the temple itself, their panels depicting the birth, death, and resurrection of Osiris.

That day now seemed part of an ancient dream, a floating collection of moments rich in texture and sweetened with the fragrance of the flowering acacias that lined the winding walkways. I waggled my head. If only I could resurrect those innocent days and anesthetize all that's occurred since the scrolls disappeared. But no, I couldn't. Instead I rode the wave of that memory back again to the Serapeum.

All the chambers house extravagant works of art, but none is more breathtaking than Serapis himself enthroned within a semi-circular alcove at the far end of the Temple Hall. He is an enormous, exquisitely sculpted statue of marble adorned with gold plate, precious stones, and gem-chiseled ivory. Seated in profound majesty, he is lavishly bearded and robed, serene and self-centered, handsome in the Greek tradition. In his left hand, he's holding the scepter of power; in his right, he's restraining Cerberus, the three-headed dog who guards the gates of Hades. Each year, in a most stunning and sacred ceremony witnessed by throngs of his disciples, he's kissed by the sun when a shaft of morning light enters the sanctuary through a window at the precise angle to illuminate his lips and thereby assure Alexandrians of his continuing protection.

Papa took a long sip of his already tepid tea, preparing to continue his recall of that day. When his hand trembled, some of the tea splashed onto the table, flooding one of my swirls, and refocusing my attention onto his story.

"…proudly watching while the priest sheared each ephebe's hair, Binyamin's first, instantly transforming him into a man among boys, lean, broad-shouldered, and magnetic, someone Emperor Claudius would enroll in the order of the Equestrians."

Papa paused again, this time to gaze into the moonlight. While I pretended to nibble on a cinnamon cake, his hard swallows told me he was feeling the memory viscerally. When he continued, his voice dipped into a moan as thick and distant as the muffled rumble of the sea.

"But then came that day at the Gymnasium's *palaistra*, his first *pankration* bout, when he slew young Titus. I knew at that moment that no matter how hard I would try to keep the promise I made to your mother, Binyamin would be the athlete more than the scholar, a Greek more than a Jew, or worse yet, a Roman, barbarous, haughty, and determined to win at all costs."

Papa pressed his lips together and tightened his grip on the glass.

"The horror of that day turned my fatherly pride into disgust, and he became for me a grotesque caricature of his boyhood self."

I didn't have the heart to remind Papa that he'd been rejecting Binyamin long before young Titus's death. Instead I said, "Papa, your tea is getting cold" and shifted the conversation to the present.

"Maybe the lesson, Papa, is that, notwithstanding a parent's well-intentioned guidance, children have to define their own future. As a parent you gave Binyamin the opportunity for a wide range of choices. Then it was up to him to choose the life that made the most sense to him."

I paused so he could grasp my meaning. When he leaned back, put his glass down, and folded his arms across his chest, I continued.

"Just as Binyamin has chosen a life, I have to choose one as well. You've showered me with all I could want: a loving and gracious home, a tutor like Hector, and a devoted friend like Phoebe—and even Noah—but now I must make my own choices."

Still, I could hear my all-too-familiar placatory singsong, and I despised it. The time had come to banish the actress who, masquerading as my double, had been playing the role of his submissive daughter. Hadn't I spent the better part of the week surmounting my fears? Could my father pose a greater threat to me than the pitiless streets of the *Rhakotis* Quarter?

Still, the finger of fear pressed against my throat. I stared into the tallow lamp and for courage, imagined myself married to Noah, enduring his fawning apologies, his blatant ogles, his feverish lips pouring his sour vapor into me, his putrid odor fouling my skin. And me, claustrophobic in his embrace, doomed to miss the ecstasy of erotic love.

Pulling my eyes from the lamp's writhing flame, I faced Papa squarely, drew in a ragged breath, and opened my mouth, half expecting my jaw to screech like a rickety gate.

Instead the words slid out as if they'd been waiting on my tongue for years.

"I'm not going to marry Noah. I know how much he means to you, and he can still be the son to you that you'd like him to be, but I'm not going to marry him."

There. I said what was on my mind before the opportunity had passed and I'd have in its wake only my imaginary reenactments and regrets.

I expected to see Papa's eyes blaze, his nostrils flare, his face discolor, and a plume of fire shoot from his mouth.

Instead he sat very still.

We both did.

At last he said, "Oh."

Just that one word.

He didn't speak again for several minutes. He dropped his eyelids, lowered his chin, slumped forward, and kneaded his temples. When he finally raised his lids, I could see that remorse had settled over him.

"Miriam, I've been an overbearing father to you as well as Binyamin. I've reacted out of loneliness and the fear that each of you would choose a life I didn't understand and couldn't protect you from, and most of all, a life that would exclude me. Even though I knew at the time I shouldn't burden you with my obsessions, my demons goaded me. Later, I would spend sleepless nights in self-castigation and fantasy conversations to convince myself that you would someday be better off. I knew I shouldn't be forcing you or Binyamin to choose between your filial obligations and your destiny, that I couldn't mitigate your destinies anyway—your mother's astrologer explained that before you were even born—but the fear of losing you and Binyamin, after having lost your mother, fanned my anguish like an irrepressible wind."

Looking back, I realized I'd been waiting years for this admission.

"I understand, Papa. I always have. I never thought you meant to hurt us, but I hope someday you'll have the chance to explain this to Binyamin."

Feeling now more like his parent than his child, I peeled his fingers from the glass and grasped his hand.

"No matter what I do, Papa, no matter where I go, the bond between us is secure. For now, I will continue to work with you, to assist you in your business and manage our home, but my goal is to study alchemy, whether or not I ever recover the scrolls. I want to learn how to perfect the spirit of metals and develop the recipes, procedures, and apparatus to work with them safely. And I want to learn how to perfect the human spirit as well."

The flickering light of the tallow lamp caught the moisture in his eyes. He tried to blink back the tears, so I looked up at the ferns as if distracted by their baskets swaying in the sea breeze.

But then my focus returned to the immediate and the lie I'd been living as Noah's betrothed. "I'll go see Noah tomorrow to explain why he must free me from the marriage contract." I had to see him before *Shabbat*. I could no longer go through the charade of another day as his betrothed, and once *Shabbat* arrives, the discussion of all disagreeable matters is forbidden.

So with that announcement, I drained my glass, set it firmly on its saucer, and bid him a good night. When I got up, I realized I was leaving behind the girl who would rather live a lie than risk a confrontation, that I was entering a new stage of life, that nothing would ever be the same. Even the moonlight had changed to a silvery, more luminous blue; the sea breeze, to a fresh-scented wash over my skin. And to my astonishment, I discovered a spring in my stride, as if I were bounding through the aether, no longer compelled to count the steps back to my suite.

Chapter 27

Early Friday Morning

WITH SO MUCH to do to prepare for *Shabbat*, I typically got up early every Friday morning. But on that particular Friday, my last day to recover the scrolls before having to face Judah empty-handed, I sprang out of bed before dawn. On any other Friday, I might have wriggled down between the sheets to listen to the last breath of the night wind and the chink and tinkle of crockery and cutlery as the cook prepared breakfast. But this morning, I was frantic. I had to speak with Aunt Hannah.

Besides, I couldn't have slept anyway, with so many shrill images churning in my head. Of the matrons in the quarter, their eyebrows raised, nodding slyly, and exchanging knowing looks while their malicious tongues sprayed fresh gossip about me. Of Binyamin bolting from the litter and running toward the pier. Of the hunchback slipping the letter through the thicket. Of Phoebe's seizure, Papa's contrition, and most of all, the emergence of my newly assertive self.

As my thoughts spiraled out of that tangled wasteland, I focused once again on how the thief could have smuggled the scrolls out of this house and whether Aunt Hannah would be able to substantiate my latest theory. As I figured it, the theft must have occurred last Friday evening, the only time during the window of their disappearance that someone other than Papa or Binyamin was in the library with a motive to steal them.

Namely Noah.

I found Aunt Hannah on her chaise lounge in the courtyard, a burst of light from the rising sun edging her face with a pink glow. About to breakfast on the tray before her of cantaloupe chunks dipped in yogurt, a honey muffin with raisins and walnuts, and a cup of ginger tea, she was listening to the fast, nasal-like babbling of our summer warbler. But sensing my presence, she lifted her face and turned to greet me when I sat at the foot of the adjacent chaise lounge.

"Good morning, Miriam. You're up early. Come have breakfast with me and tell me what our songbird is doing."

"At the moment, Auntie, she's perched in the thistle undergrowth on her little gray legs, about to skewer a cricket with her pointed bill. She, like you, is ready to enjoy a hardy breakfast."

But, jittery with anticipation, my stomach queasy, and my eyes gritty from sleeplessness, I shrank from the thought of eating as if a cockroach had been swimming in her tea. So I changed the subject.

"You know, Auntie, I have yet to recover the scrolls, but I've been making progress. I can't explain it fully yet, but I think Noah took them last Friday evening, and you can help me figure out how he could have done it. Remember, I wrapped him in his himation that night, escorted him to our door, and watched him turn the corner toward his house. So I know he didn't have the scrolls then."

My aunt drew in her lower lip and furrowed her brow in total concentration.

"Miriam, tell me why you think Noah took them."

"He knew I was drawn to alchemy and at the same time pulling away from him, and he knew the theft of the scrolls would discredit me with the League. Perhaps he thought the humiliation would propel me toward marrying him. He might have also caught the rumor Binyamin heard in the quarter that I'd been dallying in the agora with a new sweetheart.

"Perhaps I should be grateful that he'd still want to marry me in the wake of such gossip, but instead I'm incensed that he'd use trickery to manipulate me."

I didn't mention to Aunt Hannah that I'd had enough manipulation from Papa to last me a lifetime.

First, I needed to know whether Noah could have taken the

scrolls while Papa and Binyamin were arguing. Aunt Hannah recalled the three of them sitting around the cherry wood table. She said Noah was closest to but with his back to the cabinet. Papa was a quarter turn to Noah's right and facing her. Having just finished playing the cithara, she was still sitting in her spindly-legged chair. And Binyamin was facing Noah and the Etruscan vases. So the scrolls were only an arm's length from Noah while Papa and Binyamin were arguing.

Next, I needed to know whether Noah could have taken the scrolls into the courtyard.

"Auntie, did you happen to hear Noah wander into the courtyard during Papa and Binyamin's quarrel?" No one would have found Noah's absenting himself from a family squabble remarkable, but maybe Aunt Hannah noticed not only that he'd gotten up but where he'd gone.

Before answering, she nodded, found her cup, and took a sip of tea.

"I certainly heard him walking about. His gait is unmistakable and was especially awkward that evening, perhaps because he'd had too much wine while we were waiting for Amram. Which reminds me, Miriam, you seem to be favoring your left side this morning."

I was too impatient to detail my nocturnal adventures in the *Rhakotis* Quarter, so I told her I'd tripped and let it go at that.

"But can you tell me, Auntie, whether he walked around during the argument, and if so, whether he wandered into the courtyard?"

Putting her cup back on the tray, she pursed her lips to think and then shook her head.

"No, Miriam. I can't. I was riveted on the animosity between your Papa and Binyamin and the threat beyond *Shabbat* to the peace of this household."

She didn't say Noah entered the courtyard, but he could have. She wasn't sure. But I was. So sure that, like a scene illuminated by lightning, I could picture him reaching back into my cubby, snatching the scrolls, hiding them behind his back, slinking behind Papa, slipping into the courtyard, weaving around the island of trees toward the side street, leaning over the bed of poppies, poking the scrolls one by one through the fence, listening for each to drop into the thicket, and then returning to the library just as Binyamin was decimating Papa's Etruscan vase collection.

No wonder Noah looked feverish. But whether genuine or a sham, his headache was the perfect excuse to leave early without Amram. After rounding the corner of our side street, he would have only had to squat at the curb and reach into the thicket to retrieve the scrolls. And as he pulled each one from the undergrowth, he would have scratched his right forearm on the sharp thistle leaves just as the hunchback had.

Not exactly an attack by a pack of ravenous hounds.

A combustible rage bubbled through me. Springing off the chaise lounge as if it were a bed of burning coals, I bolted out of the courtyard, dashed through the dining room, darted past the pool, bounded out the double doors, and charged down the steps.

The familiar landmarks streaked by as I raced toward Noah's house like a runner in the pentathlon. I sprinted into the teeth of the sea breeze, its grit parching the inside of my mouth, my tunic whipping about my ankles, my hair splayed in all directions. I pleaded with myself to slow down so I could reach his house with some semblance of poise, but my legs had their own idea.

Chapter 28

Late Friday Morning

I RACED TOWARD Noah's house propelled by raw rage, my fists clenched, my arms pumping, my heart hammering, my mind whirling, my body awash in a cold sweat despite the molten sun burning through my tunic. At the same time, I sensed the three white-robed Fates nodding in satisfaction as they watched my head bobbing above the hedges, as if they'd long been drawing me to this time and place.

After a stumble and a spill—the ribbon lacing one of my sandals had snapped—I scrambled to my feet, brushed off the dust, and tossed my shoes. Still, my run was hardly slower now as my legs scissored past stables and groves, synagogues and villas, inns and restaurants, cookshops and *kapeleia*. Scores of grasshoppers snapped their wings to flee from my thunder, while the soles of my feet felt the sting of every nettle, the edge of every stone, the scratch of every briar, the prick of every splinter, and the puncture of every thorn as they pounded against the scorching sand and the razor-sharp spikes of dry yellow grass. My head throbbing, my chest heaving, my stomach twisting, my lungs screaming, my throat constricted, my legs thick, my feet bleeding, I panted toward Noah's house, all the while repeating to myself that I had nothing to be afraid of. Nothing.

Until I approached the mansion.

Its symmetry more daunting than ever.

My courage curdled when I saw its brooding, wasp-infested plane trees huddled against the outside world. With their gnarled trunks groaning, their boughs twitching, their limbs moaning, their twigs nodding, and their leaves whispering, I knew they were conspiring to block my claim to the scrolls and deny me relief from the marriage contract. As I advanced toward the grand entryway, its pilasters sneered at me. Dread consumed me. What if Noah refuses to give me the scrolls? What if he's destroyed them? What if he just folds his arms and purses his lips in mock patience when I ask him for a divorce?

I heard myself hollering for Noah, hardly believing I was that madwoman, uncombed and unkempt, banging her fists against the door, smashing her knuckles on its metal studs. But Myron opened the door promptly. If he was startled by my appearance, his wooden face hid any sign, so much so that I might have wondered whether I'd often gone there so disheveled.

Still, he must have hesitated, because I found myself hurtling past him toward Noah's suite—his sitting room, *cubiculum*, and peristyle—Myron lagging behind, hustling to keep up with me rather than the other way around. I cut around the atrium's pool and statues, charging through its cloud of aromatic oils, its onyx tiles cool against the raw soles of my feet. Which way to go? I rushed past a bank of tall, arched, unglazed windows, their shutters open to a thick grove of roses, their blossoms fusing into a single red blanket while the breeze buffeted the slippery drapes and fanned the rich floral scent. I darted down one corridor, its ceiling vaulted, its white travertine walls lined with cages of parrots and talking crows, planters of clipped boxwood, and rosewood tables bearing basins of lavender incense.

And then, recognizing the entrance to Noah's suite, I hammered on his door while shouting in a voice too hoarse for even me to recognize, "Noah! Noah, let me in!"

Breaking every rule of modesty and restraint, I barged into what used to be his sitting room but now appeared to be something quite different.

The arched ceiling was still embellished with gilded motifs of animals in light relief but was now stained yellow and shadowed with soot. Frescoes of the Great Harbor, the Pharos

Lighthouse, and the gardens of Point Lochias still decorated the walls, but his furnishings—the leather-cushioned couches and occasional chairs, the gold-handled, burled mahogany desk stacked with his own made-to-order sheets of center-cut papyrus, and the freestanding brass candelabra and terracotta statues—had been jammed in front of them.

I must have noticed these changes the moment I opened the door, because once I entered, I had to choke my way through the noxious haze. The smoke burned my eyes, blistered my skin, and settled on my lips with a nasty sting. The room had been sealed against the light of day, its long windows shut and shrouded by their deeply folded drapes. But through the lurid light of a single oil lamp, I saw that his long, narrow ebony table, once flanked by padded benches but still dominating the center of the room, was now equipped as a makeshift laboratory.

And I saw the scrolls, all three of them at the head of the table, two in the very basket I'd filled with food and given him last *Shabbat*. Mine and the League's notes from Aristotle's *Meteorologica* were rolled up, each tied with its silk sash, but the scroll with Judah and Saul's recipe for extracting mercury and perfecting copper lay unfurled across the table.

The source of the toxic fumes was in the center of the table, an open vessel of crushed cinnabar roasting over the twisting flame of the oil lamp. The inverted cup Noah had mounted above the reaction vessel to collect and condense the mercury vapors was too high to prevent the poison from seeping into the room.

Noah! Where was he?

I heard his gasps for the little air left in the room before I saw him stooped behind one of the couches, gagging and retching into a chamber pot.

In what order I cannot say, but I spun around.

Screamed for Myron.

Extinguished the oil lamp.

Smashed a statue.

Jammed its base into the mouth of the reaction vessel.

And tore down the drapes.

An explosion of sunlight bleached the room.

I shattered countless panes with the head of the statue until I could spot the door to the peristyle and fling it open. Then I ran to Noah. Leaning into his back, threading my hands under his armpits and locking them across his chest, I started to drag him outside. But with his spasms and my own shortness of breath, my balance grew untrustworthy. My arms gave out and my legs buckled just as Myron materialized at my side. He lifted Noah, and carrying him like a rag doll into the fresh air, he spread him out on a chaise lounge.

"Myron! Get a physician! Hurry!"

Poised on the edge of Noah's chaise lounge, I crouched to embrace him, looking now so skeletal, his bones protruding from his body as if they were about to pierce his skin. Reaching up, he hung his arms around my neck, and clinging, he sobbed into my shoulder, dribbling a frothy pink sputum that trickled down my chest. His shallow, irregular breaths whistled in his chest as though the air were trapped in a cage and pressing to escape, but each pant only triggered another round of loud, productive coughs. Then, wincing as he lay back, his nostrils flared, his eyes filmy, his teeth rimmed in red, his mushroom-colored face hollow, he clawed the air to bring my ear to his lips. He whispered haltingly, releasing his words with a gurgle as if he were underwater, but his mind seemed clear.

"Mimi, I took your scrolls. Please, my darling, forgive me. I've caused you so much worry. I wanted to be like Judah—I know who he is, Mimi, that you've been spending time with him. I wanted to learn about his experiments, to study alchemy so you would forget about him and love me again. I've felt the coolness between us. I know I've been too busy with work. My father's been too distraught to carry his share of the partnership. I've neglected you so. Oh, Mimi, I'm so sorry. Please forgive me."

His voice was thick with remorse.

For a few moments he drifted into a distant reality, but after another round of wet coughs, he stifled the pain and gulping between sobs, managed to murmur, "I planned to surprise you with what I've learned, but I never imagined the disappearance of the scrolls would distress you so. When you came to me so upset, I was too afraid to confess, too afraid of losing you. I could never survive losing you, Mimi. Never."

A rush of bile scorched my innards. Why in G-d's name couldn't I have just married him?

"So I figured I'd return the scrolls this evening when I came for *Shabbat*. Maybe I'd bring them in a different basket hidden under some flasks of wine from Palestine, as though I were bringing you a gift and at the same time, replacing the basket you gave me last *Shabbat*. Or maybe I'd walk over alone, and with a fresh bandage to protect my forearm, I'd plant the scrolls at the base of the thicket. Then, excusing myself for a few minutes during dinner, I'd reach through the fence, retrieve them, and put them back in your cubby."

His confession brought him some relief. His body relaxed, and his breathing eased.

"But Noah, my scroll has the directions for collecting the mercury vapors safely. Why didn't you follow them? And why were your windows and drapes closed? The smoke could have suffocated you."

"I tried to follow them, but they were confusing, incomplete, even cryptic, as if you'd written them that way deliberately"—

How could Noah have known that we protect our experimental secrets that way?

"—Quite unlike you, Mimi. Besides, who'd have thought the fumes would be so vile?"

That's Noah, believing that his wealth makes him invincible, especially against anything as amorphous as a vapor.

"—And I wanted to keep my experiments private, at least until I could surprise you and so no one could spy on me. I remembered how important you said it was to protect the secrets in these scrolls.

"Mimi, tell me you forgive me and that we can be married soon."

Another rush of bile, this one surging up my gorge, burning my throat, stinging my mouth, and coating my tongue with slime.

He took my hand and squeezed it, but once again, his eyes clouded over, his lids drooped, his grip relaxed, and he drifted away. When his cough returned, it was more virulent than ever, a wracking, hacking, chest-rattling, ear-grating, convulsive cough, culminating in a violent fit of gags and heaves as plumes of a crimson lava gushed from his mouth, cascading down the front of my tunic and painting the polished floor tiles red.

"Noah!"

And then he was silent.

Choking.

Clutching this throat.

His eyes first pleading, then bulging, frantic.

His mouth open, twisting in a silent scream.

His tongue fighting the obstruction.

His complexion blanching.

The semicircles under his eyes darkening.

Fast.

I tilted his head back, and holding open his mouth, I reached inside to the back of his throat, sweeping through the effluence with my index finger, probing for the obstruction in his airway. I picked out some unidentifiable chunks of partially-digested food but nothing more before he slipped into unconsciousness.

"Noah, please." Then louder, "Noah, breathe."

I pounded his chest, but he stared past me, his eyes opaque.

I grasped his shoulders and shook him, but he paid me no mind.

I pulled him to a sitting position, but his head just flopped over.

I slapped his back, but he folded forward.

I shouted in his ear. "Noah, please, one more breath."

But he couldn't hear me.

He'd already surrendered his connection to this world and crossed into the World- to-Come.

So I lowered him back onto the chaise lounge.

I squatted beside him, closing his translucent lids, caressing his still-warm face, bending his elbows, and folding his arms across his chest as if they were the fragile wings of a wounded bird. And I thought with shame how much easier he is to love like this.

With his confession, my rage had given way to guilt. What's more, the guilt was suffused with shock, even panic. How would I ever cope without him? Who else could read my every nuance? Who else even cared to? True, I hadn't wanted to marry him, but I still pictured our growing old together. I counted on his friendship to sustain me, especially after Binyamin's departure, to share the memories of our childhood, even to lavish me with compliments when I looked and felt my worst. And who else could advise my father about our investments?

But to my shame, the guilt, shock, and panic were marbled with relief, as if a storm had just passed, its thunderheads having given way to fans of sunlight to dry the rain-soaked landscape. Nonetheless, I beat my chest for having trifled so long with his affection, wishing like a foolish child I could turn the time back to last Friday. Why couldn't I have declared my intention then of breaking the marriage contract, first with Papa and then with Noah, before he took the scrolls? That question would inhabit my body like a ghost.

Otherwise, I felt detached, as if I were looking down on someone else's drama, observing a woman who only looked like me as she knelt caressing the brow of a prone statue. Or perhaps I was there but only as an actress playing that woman's part. Or best yet, while waiting for Noah, I'd fallen into a scene from a Tartarean dream. When he returns, I thought, he'll awaken me. Then we'll sip cinnamon tea while he chides me for having let it steep too long. We'll munch on sugared almonds while the breeze fans the scent of the flowering oleander and cools the ferns arching over their hanging baskets.

Can it be that Noah has really left this world? That he'll never again dine with us on *Shabbat*, read to me from *Aesop's Fables*, welcome me with his toothy smile, tell me I'm beautiful when I'm disheveled, or grouse about Alexandria's political corruption, violence, extravagant festivals, lascivious entertainers, cloying beggars, or clamorous street philosophers? Impossible. Not with the honeyed light of this ordinary day. Not with the skipper butterflies darting above us. Not with the hum of the bees, the burble of the fountains, and the mumble of the leaves beyond the peristyle. No, it cannot be.

But if he's still among us, then why are his lips colorless and his nail beds gray? Why has his body turned to wax, his skin to paste? And why is he deaf to my words? I cast about for some explanation while taking a few deep breaths to confirm that I myself was still alive.

The impossible had happened, and I couldn't undo it. Rocking backward onto my heels and straightening up, tottering as if the horizon had tilted, I steadied myself on the arm of the chaise lounge while beads of sweat from the back of my knees trickled down my calves. I staggered back into Noah's sitting room, reeling from a wave of dizziness, and forged a path through the wreckage, through the smithereens of broken glass and the islets of torn drapes, all the while my eyes smarting as I held my breath against the toxic vapors. Heading straight for the table, I grabbed the open scroll, rolled it up pell-mell, and scooped up the other two. I carried them like infants in my arms as I brushed past the foot of the table, closed the door, heard the click of the latch, and set out to find Amram.

Chapter 29

Early Friday Evening

WAS IT ONLY last week that I was positioning not just two but all three of these couches in an arc facing the courtyard, running my hands over their woodwork and plumping their cushions? Was it only last *Shabbat* that I was listening to Papa first bait Noah and then Binyamin while they waited in the library for Amram? As I prepared to serve *Shabbat* dinner to Papa, Aunt Hannah, and myself, the dining room seemed oddly bare, the air static as if no one lived here anymore. That and a queer chill were all I felt as I directed my limbs to perform the routines that even a crisis cannot subvert.

Throughout that afternoon, whenever I'd relive the morning's calamity, fresh tears would burn a salty trail down my face and spill onto my tunic. Others would cling to my cheeks and sting like beads of acid. Amram had been at the Gymnasium, so I'd sent his bearers to fetch him. Surely he had an inkling that something was dreadfully wrong when Myron, in the absence of Noah, settled him with a goblet of wine on a bench in the atrium.

I'd been waiting in the courtyard, re-rolling the scrolls, checking them for damage while trying to compose myself and rehearse some comforting words for Amram. But when I entered the atrium and sat down next to him, Myron standing behind me, I could see that Amram was already anticipating the news. With his eyelids fluttering, his lips pinched, his shoulders hunched, and his chin pressed to his chest, he was rocking back and forth, his arms folded across his lap, one hand dangling the goblet, the last of its contents bleeding into the seams between the tiles.

Taking hold of his goblet and handing it to Myron, I grasped Amram's bloodless hands—they felt like sheaths of desiccated papyrus—and pressed them between my own. I mumbled something—I can't remember what I'd memorized—but I needn't have bothered. When Amram raised his head and saw my crimson-soaked tunic and shock-filled eyes, he knew. That's when the pain ripped through his body, when he released an unearthly wail that reverberated through the house, when his eyes clamped shut and his face contorted in anguish, when his body folded over and crumpled to the floor. He'd been gored, but his soul not his blood was spurting from the wound.

In spite of the showy blossoms floating in the pool, the beds of irises along its perimeter, and the bouquets of freshly-cut roses pluming over their free-standing urns, the atrium, like Amram, had lost all its color. Myron carried his broken master to bed, the shallow rise and fall of Amram's chest the only sign he was still alive.

I sent Amram's bearers to the *Bruchium* Quarter again, this time to Aspasia's for an extract of mandrake root. Then, retracing my steps through the maze of corridors to the courtyard, I grabbed from one of the tables a long, oval basket, its handle arched over sprays of budding lavender. I distributed the sprays among the other baskets and brought the now empty basket to the courtyard, where I packed it with the scrolls. Threading one arm through its handle and cradling it against my hip, I toddled home on swollen feet while my head wagged in disbelief, my stomach churned with guilt, and my ears buzzed with the kind of shameful excitement that follows a tragedy when it's not your own.

Objects clattered in my wake as I lumbered about the house in the fading afternoon light to complete the *Shabbat* preparations. I'd feel anesthetized and think I'd reached the point when I could weep no more only to find my cheeks wet again. Fresh waves of grief and guilt, remorse and recrimination, would flood me with the memory of Noah's last breath, his plea for forgiveness without an iota of reproach for my having seeded the gossip that propelled him to take the scrolls.

Aunt Hannah was in the library. She'd been playing her cithara but must have heard some moths fluttering against the window pane, because she put it aside, my signal to prepare my spirit to welcome *Shabbat*. I blessed G-d for being the Creator of life even in the face of Noah's death. Then I inserted the candles in my mother's candlesticks and lit them to usher in the sacred day. Reassured by this familiar ritual, I added my own prayers to the traditional blessing:

"May Noah's soul, sheltered by Your divine wings, be treasured among the souls of his mother, sisters, and all the other righteous people who merit a place in the World-to-Come. And may You comfort Amram as he mourns the loss of his only son.

"May You grant me the strength to safeguard the League's sacred secrets for the Seed of Abraham, Your Chosen People, so that the vulgar and ignorant cannot pervert Your Great Work. May You lead me on a journey toward spiritual purity so that I might, in memory of Noah, merit Your Holy Insights and so perfect the bodies and spirits of base metals along with those of all the people who are sick. And may You teach me to be compassionate, especially toward those who have entrusted me with their love."

As I concluded my prayers, I resolved that as soon as *Shabbat* was over, I would construct and test the apparatus for vaporizing and condensing mercury that I'd detailed in my scroll so that others would not die as Noah did.

And then I heard a voice in the atrium.

"Please, Mr. ben Asher, may I speak with Miriam?"

Only one voice could seize me like that.

The heels of Judah's boots cut a staccato rhythm across the mosaic tiles.

Papa ushered him into the dining room. I hoped he was coming for the scrolls, that Saul's condition had improved enough for him to have asked Judah for them.

But no. Judah's mournful face told me otherwise.

When he looked at me, a fleeting squint creased his face. He must have noticed the bruises on my face, the discolorations more a yellowish green today than yesterday's flamboyant purple. I felt a blush creep up my neck, but as soon as he spoke, it receded.

"Miriam, Saul passed away late this afternoon. The boy is staying with him until after *Shabbat*, when the undertaker will prepare his body for burial Sunday morning."

Then, noticing the *Shabbat* candles, he raked his hands through his hair and turned to Papa.

"I beg your pardon, Mr. ben Asher. I didn't mean to interrupt *Shabbat*. I got here as soon as I could, but I see *Shabbat* arrived before I did."

A heavy silence threatened to fill the room.

But Papa dipped his head in a slight nod and twitched a tight smile. "You're welcome to stay, Judah."

Then, looking at me, Papa gestured expansively and cleared his throat as if to address an audience. "Miriam, please ask Phoebe to make a place for Judah in the dining room."

"Come, Judah," I said, taking pleasure as I heard his name from my own lips. "Let me seat you in the courtyard while Phoebe prepares the dining room."

I accompanied him to a chaise lounge just as an opalescent sky was settling into layers of lavender, lilac, indigo, and violet. The moon had begun its climb through the tangled net of evening stars, and the date palms and plane trees sliced the delicate light into long shadows.

With Judah seated by the fountain, I excused myself to help Phoebe reposition the third couch around the ivory table and add a place for dinner. On the way, I asked a maid to bring Judah some sesame cakes and a goblet of wine, refreshments he'd yet to touch by the time I returned to the courtyard. Instead he sat hunched forward, his mouth compressed, its corners pulled down, his hands clenched, his fingers intertwined, his brow furrowed, his eyes staring into the distance.

I perched on the edge of the chaise lounge to face him.

I unlocked his hands and held them.

Their warmth felt comfortable.

We didn't say anything for a while.

He took a deep breath that became a sigh, and when he spoke, his voice quavered. "I want to find Eran, to tell him our father has passed away."

Now I was the one to squint. "What do you mean? Saul was Eran's father, not yours."

"No, Miriam. He was my father too. He told me so shortly before he died. He might never have told me, but when I was taking care of him, I found his amulet, an exact match to mine in not only the design but the alloying of the silver and, of course, my mother's mark. So I asked him about his relationship with my mother and why he'd kept it a secret from me even after his wife died.

"He told me he was afraid that on the one hand I'd feel an obligation toward him beyond my duty as his protégé, a tribute he felt he didn't deserve. On the other hand, he was afraid I'd reject him for having been responsible for the derision my mother and I had to endure.

"He couldn't face the prospect of that rejection, especially after Eran disowned him. Somehow Eran had long suspected the affair with my mother. Although Saul denied it vehemently and repeatedly, each denial only heightened Eran's irritability and increased the acrimony between them. Saul was afraid that if he did acknowledge the affair, Eran might, in a fit of indignation, hurl the painful truth at his mother and thereby exacerbate her mania. What's more, his acknowledgment, he said, could precipitate a manic episode in Eran himself. According to Saul, Eran, like his mother years ago, had begun to exhibit periods of heightened impulsiveness, belligerence, even delusions. Saul was afraid that during such an episode, Eran might fixate on identifying and punishing the woman he saw as violating the sanctity of his family and arrogating his father's affection.

"And, of course, Saul was ashamed of himself, ashamed that he'd betrayed his wife, that he hadn't shared in our humiliation, and after Dinah's passing, that he'd continued to withhold the truth from me.

"Anyway, Eran left Alexandria almost fifteen years ago. Saul figured he became a jeweler. At least he began to train with one in Judea. He never came back to Alexandria, and Saul never heard a word from or about him again. He had no idea where Eran was or even what name he could be using. All he had was a vague idea of what Eran might look like—Eran was born with a port-wine stain across his forehead—and that he'd be twenty-eight years old.

"So, I know I have a brother, and I want to find him."

I sat with him in silence, the prick of tears gathering behind my eyes and tightening my throat.

I LAY ON MY sleeping couch that night with Phoebe kneeling on the pallet beside me, listening to my lament and reaching up to wipe each tear before it could trickle through my hair. Later, between gusts of grief, when I felt strangely composed, I vowed to the Almighty that before too many days had smudged the details, I would record the events of this past week for young women everywhere. Let them see that I lived the deadliest lie, pretending to be Noah's betrothed, and now must bear the responsibility for his death as surely as if I'd unleashed the poisonous vapors myself. Let them judge me, even blame me, but above all let them learn from me so they too can claim their future, but forthrightly, without the trail of harm I've caused.

Epilogue

One Year Later

AS I READ THIS, my completed manuscript, I'm surprised by what I've written, even astonished by how much I managed to recall. Still, I'm sorry I didn't express more appreciation for Papa and Noah: Papa for his staunch desire to protect and provide for us—not only me but Binyamin and, of course, Aunt Hannah—and Noah for his steadfast and unconditional love. Henceforth I'll try to be more mindful of their virtues. Otherwise, I'm content to let this account of that terrible week stand.

This past year has been the traditional mourning period for me, Noah's betrothed, as well as for Amram. Despite his seclusion, Amram has welcomed the men from the Synagogue who, along with Papa, have formed the minyan for his daily prayers. And he's looked forward to my visits every Friday, to our sharing the afternoon's last light. In addition to bringing him a *Shabbat* dinner, some mandrake root, and news of Philo, all of which would lift his spirits, I'd light his candles to usher in the peace of *Shabbat*. After that, if he felt up to chatting, he'd reminisce about the sweet *Shabbatot* he'd spent as a student, young husband, and father.

I'll continue to remember Amram in my daily prayers and visit him, though not so regularly now as I work to carve a worthwhile life out of the misfortune I've caused. This past year I experimented with metal, clay, and glass to construct the apparatus for safely condensing the vapors of mercury in accord with the design I recorded just before Noah took the scrolls. I've named the apparatus Noah's Still, but because it's a modification of the *kerotakis*, the charcoal burner artists have been using for centuries to keep their paints from hardening, my colleagues in the League persist in referring to it by that more familiar name.

I've also made a more complex still by inserting three copper tubes into an earthenware flask and sealing the joints with flour paste. And I've been mixing the juice of jellyfish with the gall of tortoises to enhance the luminosity of precious stones, all for the glory of G-d. May He continue to instruct me in His divine art while sheltering Noah under His heavenly wings.

With gratitude to Our Creator,

The seal of Miriam bat Isaac
Alexandria *ad Aegyptum*
Summer of the Seventh Year of the Reign of Tiberius Claudius Caesar Augustus Germanicus [Claudius]

Author's Note

Maria Hebrea lived. I first encountered a reference to her work more than twenty years ago in a course on the historical development of concepts in chemistry. I wondered how a Jewish woman from Ancient Alexandria became the legendary founder of Western alchemy and held her place for 1500 years as the most celebrated woman of the Western World. Who was she, and what was her life like?

And who were the early alchemists? I'd previously thought of them as inconsequential dreamers or misguided mystics—if not sorcerers or downright charlatans—attempting to do what anybody else should know was impossible. But if they were experimental scientists, then what theories guided their attempts to transmute base metals into silver and gold? These questions continued to intrigue me.

I've called her Miriam bat Isaac, but no one knows what her name was or even when she lived. In fact, no one knows anything about her personal life except that she was a fervent Jewess (Patai, 1994). None of her contemporaries wrote about her or her work. We only know the theories and inventions other alchemists attributed to her long after her time. One such alchemist, Zosimos of Panopolis, who lived near the end of the third or the beginning of the fourth century and authored the earliest-known books on alchemy, cited her as the ultimate age-old authority (Leicester, 1971; Patai, 1994).

In the alchemical literature, Maria Hebrea is also referred to as Mary the Jewess or Miriam the Prophetess, sister of Moses. Like her, all alchemists wrote under the name of a deity, prophet, or philosopher from an earlier time perhaps to enhance the authenticity of their claims or shield themselves from persecution. Although the tradition among all the crafts and mystical cults at the time was to guard the secrecy of their work, persecution was a real risk for alchemists.

By the end of the third century, the work of the Alexandrian alchemists had become sufficiently well known for the falsification of gold to be regarded as a threat to the stability of the currency. Consequently, Emperor Diocletian ordered the burning of all alchemical books in 292 CE (Leiscester, 1971). And so the creative period of Alexandrian alchemy came to an end. Although the Arabs managed to rescue some of the books—they had long venerated Maria Hebrea and her alchemical theories—by the time the books had been copied, recopied, transmitted through the geographic expansion of the early Church, and rediscovered in the monasteries of medieval Europe, the lore had been reduced to charlatanism.

Maria Hebrea lived in Alexandria, the center of Hellenistic culture, the intellectual melting pot of Greek philosophy, Eastern mysticism, and Egyptian technology. In Alexandria, the practical knowledge of metallurgists merged with the theories of Aristotle, in particular his theory of the Unity of Nature, the idea that all materials are composed of variant forms of the same vital substance. Accordingly, alchemists inferred that just as a sick (imperfect) human body can be transmuted into a healthy (perfect) one by the addition of some extract of this vital substance, a sick (imperfect) metal like copper can likewise be transmuted into a healthy (perfect) one, namely silver or gold. When they recognized that their alloys were less than perfect, they still believed that with better methods and the moral purity to merit G-d's grace (earned through performing good deeds), they could transmute (heal) the metal into a perfect one.

The first alchemists were Jews. They alone possessed the sacred knowledge (Patai, 1994). In its earliest days, alchemy was a spiritual as well as a material quest for perfection. The goal was to perfect all souls, the souls of humans as well as the souls of metals. Maria Hebrea regarded metals as living (and dying) and having male and female parts with the potential in her laboratory at least metaphorically to sexually generate the perfect metal. But the objective of most alchemists was more practical: to invent less expensive ways to obtain silver and gold, fabricate pearls, to add luminosity to precious stones, and to produce all kinds of tinctures and dyes. Inasmuch as many alchemists were physicians, they also sought to identify and prepare remedies for every known disease and, most important, to create the ultimate elixir to heal, rejuvenate, and extend human life.

Scholars agree on the nature of early alchemy but differ as to when Maria Hebrea lived. Some place her as having lived as early as 200 BCE (Hauck, 2008) or as late as 300 CE (Patai, 1994). But in accord with Lindsay (1970), I've placed her in the first century CE, when Alexandria was at its intellectual zenith and Western alchemy flourished (Leicester, 1971). Later, Roman superstition, magic, and mysticism would displace experimentation as a way to understand the material world, an intellectual shift evident in the texts of Zosimos. In particular, I've set the story in 46 CE so my character would have a memory of the Pogrom of 38 and that memory would justify her alarm over the theft of the scrolls and her fear that the dissemination of their secrets beyond "the seed of Abraham" (Patai, 1994) would incite another pogrom.

Scholars also differ on some of the details I've incorporated into my story. For example, did Ptolemy IX replace Alexander's gold coffin with one of crystal (Pollard & Reid, 2006), alabaster (Casson, 1994), or glass (Marlowe, 1971)? Were the Canopic Way and the Street of the Soma over 100 feet wide (Vrettos, 2001), almost 100 feet wide (Lewis, 1983; Strabo, as quoted in Jones, 1932), or 46 feet wide (De Camp, 1972)? Could building construction have progressively narrowed these streets (McKenzie, 2007)?

Sly (1995) says the first-century Canopic Way was paved with rectangular blocks. Marlowe (1971) says the blocks were grayish stone squares. Pollard and Reid (2006) say the blocks were granite. Lewis (1983) says the streets were paved with cobblestones, but De Camp (1972) says the streets may not have been paved at all. Would Maria Hebrea have had to climb one hundred (Parsons, 1967) or two hundred (Marlowe, 1971) steps to reach the quadrangle at the summit of the Serapeum? Was Serapis made of marble (Parsons, 1967; Sly, 1995) or wood (Marlowe, 1971)?

Likewise, scholars differ as to the precise location of the Museum and Great Library, as well as the relative locations of the *Heptastadion*, the agora, and the warehouse district. All of them locate the Museum and Great Library at the intersection of the Canopic Way and the Street of the Soma. But did the campus occupy the northwest (Marlowe, 1971), northeast (Sly, 1995) or southwest corner (Empereur, 1998)? Did the *Heptastadion* connect Pharos Island to Alexandria's agora (Marlowe, 1971) or warehouse district (Sly, 1995)? Inasmuch as wars, earthquakes, and earthquake subsidence destroyed much of Ancient Alexandria, and the silting of the Nile has been altering the coastline for millennia, we can be grateful to Strabo, Philo, and others for their elaborate and otherwise mutually consistent descriptions of their splendid city.

So how much of my story is factual? The accounts of or about Alexander the Great, the Ptolemies (including Cleopatra), Mark Antony, the Roman emperors, Flaccus, and Philo are congruent with the historical record. To the extent that we can trust Juvenal's *Satire VI* (Green, 1999) to be an accurate depiction of the wantonness of Roman women (rather than an acidic reaction to their having invaded the world, pleasures, and privileges of men), then a senator's wife named Eppia did in fact take refuge in Alexandria with a disfigured gladiator named Sergius.

I have, however, taken liberties with Sergius. Juvenal was not born until about 55 CE and the *Satires* not written until after 100 CE, decades after my story. But otherwise, as with Sergius, the d'Anastasy connection to the story is fictitious.

The account of each of the following events is also congruent with the historical record, at least according to some scholars: the Pogrom of 38 (Allegro, 1972; Gruen, 2002), the bloody spectacle of reckless fans charging onto the track during a chariot race (Vrettos, 2001), and tax-collector brutality, including the slow, humiliating execution in the agora of a fugitive's entire family (Sly, 1995).

The rest of the characters, events, and descriptions, though narrative inventions, are also based, albeit more loosely, on the research of scholars. In particular, I've relied on the following works to depict life in Alexandria two thousand years ago:

1. Allegro, J. M. (1972). *The chosen people.* Garden City, NY: Doubleday.

2. Bowman, A. K. (1986). *Egypt after the pharaohs 332 BC—AD 642: From Alexander to the Arab conquest.* Berkeley, CA: University of California Press.

3. Casson, L. (1994). *Travel in the ancient world.* Baltimore, MD: Johns Hopkins University Press.

4. De Camp, L. S. (1972). *Great cities of the ancient world.* Garden City, NY: Doubleday.

5. Empereur, J.-Y. (1998). *Alexandria rediscovered.* New York: Braziller.

6. Green, P. (Trans.). (1999). *Juvenal: The sixteen satires* (3rd ed.). New York: Penguin.

7. Gruen, E. S. (2002). *Diaspora: Jews amidst Greeks and Romans.* Cambridge, MA: Harvard University Press.

8. Hauck, D. W. (2008). *The complete idiot's guide to alchemy.* New York: Alpha Books (Penguin).

9. Henderson, J. (Ed.). (2004). *Philo (Volume I): On the account of the world's creation given by Moses, allegorical interpretations of Genesis* (Loeb Classical Library, Vol. 1). (F. H. Colson & G. H. Whitaker, Trans.). Cambridge, MA: Harvard University Press.

10. Hengel, M. (1980). *Jews, Greeks, and barbarians: Aspects of the Hellenization of Judaism in the pre-Christian period.* Philadelphia: Fortress Press.

11. Houston, M. G. (1931). *Ancient Greek, Roman, and Byzantine costume and decoration.* London: A. & C. Black.

12. Jashemski, W. F. (1993). *The gardens of Pompeii: Herculaneum and the villas destroyed by Vesuvius* (Vol. 2). New Rochelle, NY: Aristide D. Caratzas.

13. Jones, H. L. (Trans.). (1932). *The geography of Strabo, Volume VIII, Book 17 and General Index.* (Loeb Classical Library No. 267). Cambridge, MA: Harvard University Press.

14. Kasher, A. (1995). Synagogues as "houses of prayer" and "holy places" in the Jewish communities of Hellenistic and Roman Egypt. In D. Urman & P. V. M. Flesher (Eds.), *Ancient synagogues: Historical analysis and archaeological discovery* (pp. 205-220). The Hague: Netherlands, Brill Academic Publishers.

15. Kelly, K. (2009). *The history of medicine: Early civilizations, prehistoric times to 500 CE.* New York: Facts on File.

16. Leicester, H. M. (1971). *The historical background of chemistry.* New York: Dover.

17. Le Toquin, A., & Bosser, J. (2006). *Gardens in time.* New York: Harry N. Abrams.

18. Lewis, N. (1983). *Life in Egypt under Roman rule.* New York: Oxford University Press.

19. Lindsay, J. (1970). *The origins of alchemy in Graeco-Roman Egypt.* Perth, Western Australia: Muller.

20. Marlowe, J. (1971). *The golden age of Alexandria.* London: Victor Gollancz.

21. McKenzie, J. (2007). *The architecture of Alexandria and Egypt c.300 BC—AD 700.* New Haven, CT: Yale University Press.

22. Meijer, F. (2004). *The gladiators: History's most deadly sport* (L. Waters, Trans.). New York: St. Martin's Press.

23. Parsons, E. A. (1967). *The Alexandrian Library: Glory of the Hellenic World.* Essex, England: Elsevier Publishing.

24. Patai, R. (1994). *The Jewish alchemists: A history and source book.* Princeton, NJ: Princeton University Press.

25. Pollard, J., & Reid, H. (2006). *The rise and fall of Alexandria: Birthplace of the modern mind.* New York: Viking (Penguin).

26. Pomeroy, S. B. (1981). Women in Roman Egypt: A preliminary study based on papyri. In H. P. Foley (Ed.), *Reflections of Women in Antiquity.* (pp. 303-322). New York: Gordon and Breach Science Publishers.

27. Pomeroy, S. B. (1984). *Women in Hellenistic Egypt: From Alexander to Cleopatra.* New York: Schocken Books.

28. Sly, D. I. (1995). *Philo's Alexandria.* London: Routledge.

29. Smallwood, E. M. (1976). *The Jews under Roman rule: From Pompey to Diocletian.* Leiden, the Netherlands: E. J. Brill.

30. Tcherikover, V. (1970). *Hellenistic Civilization and the Jews* (S. Applebaum, Trans.). New York: Atheneum.

31. Vrettos, T. (2001). *Alexandria: City of the Western mind.* New York: Simon & Schuster (Free Press).

Aside from the work of these scholars, I am indebted to my academic mentor, Professor Jean Lythcott, for introducing me to the study of chemistry from a historical perspective and inspiring me to learn about Maria Hebrea. I have felt Jeannie's blessings on all my work.

Further, I am grateful to Deborah Smith, my editor at Bell Bridge Books, for her enthusiasm for Miriam's story and her gentle guidance. She has made my childhood dream come true.

Every writer should have a family and friends like mine, beginning with my twin sister and earliest reader, Gail Trop Kushner, for her painstaking editing of Miriam's story. Another life-long friend, Professor Lewis M. Greenberg, an expert in art history and culture, zealously checked the accuracy of my facts. Both supported me so generously with their attention to detail. As for my other family members and friends, I'm grateful to those who had the interest to ask about the book as well as to those who had the sensitivity not to, especially as I struggled to maintain optimism in the face of a torrent of rejections, and to those who over the years did both. You know who you are.

But most of all, I thank my husband Paul. He is always here for me. He believes in me and embraces my every goal as his own.

Finally, I hope that Maria Hebrea, whoever she was, whenever she lived, and wherever she is, forgives the liberties I have taken with her life. May she recognize my profound respect for her spiritual quest and scientific accomplishments.

Glossary

abba (Hebrew) father

andabates (Latin) the event featuring more than a dozen gladiators who, wearing helmets without eyeholes, blindly brandish their swords at each other

asclepieion (Greek) a healing temple dedicated to the worship of Asclepius

birrus brittanicus (Latin) a long, woolen cloak worn with a hood to protect against the cold

cantharus (Latin) a two-handled drinking cup shaped like a bowl

capitium (Latin) a short, light chemise used as a woman's undergarment or for sleeping

centenarius (Latin) a horse that has won at least a hundred races

collegium iuvenum (Latin) a social club for training high-ranking males over the age of fourteen in the martial arts

colobium (Latin) a coarse, short-sleeved, workingman's tunic

compluvium (Latin) the open circle in the roof above the pool in the atrium

copa (Latin) a woman who runs an inn catering to sailors, carters, and slaves

cubiculum (Latin) a sleeping chamber

discuplina bona (Latin) a good disciple

exomis (Greek) a short, left-sleeved, laborer's tunic that bares the right half of the wearer's chest

falx (Latin) a knife with a curved blade and sharp inside edge used by Roman charioteers in the event of a crash to cut the reins wrapped around their waist

familia gladiatoria (Latin) the troupe of gladiators owned by a *lanista*

kapeleion (sing.), **kapeleia** (pl.) (Greek) a snack bar providing cold snacks and beverages

kerotakis (Greek) the cylindrical or spherical apparatus Maria Hebrea (known as Miriam bat Isaac in this novel) invented to vaporize and condense mercury, arsenic, or sulfur over a plate of base metal, the first step in her transmutation process.

korykos (Greek) a punch-bag room

lacerna (Latin) a long, hooded, homespun cloak typically worn by slaves

lanista (Latin) the owner and manager of a troupe of gladiators

laographia (Latin) the poll tax levied on all males 14—60 years of age except those belonging to a privileged class, e.g., Roman citizens, priests, scholars in the Museum, and non-Roman, high-ranking officials

ludus (Latin) school to train gladiators

mastigophori (Latin) the men in the arena who wield long-handled pitchforks, whips, or scourges to goad the fighters

meta (Latin) the gilded column that is the turning point for each lap of a chariot race

paenula (Latin) a semi-circular, woolen, or leather knee-length cloak worn with a hood to protect against rain

palaistra (Latin) the section of a gymnasium serving as a wrestling school and fitted with seats for spectators

pankration (Greek) a strenuous sport that combines boxing and wrestling

pantopoleion (Greek) a general store

pedisequi (Latin) the slaves who follow their master when he leaves the house. Typically they accompany his litter to secure his safety.

primus palus (Latin) literally "the first pole," the title given to the best combatants within a *ludus*

prote hyle (Greek) literally "prime matter," the blackened mass formed during the first step to transmute a base metal

retiarius (Latin) the type of gladiator specializing in a net and trident as his weaponry

rudis (Latin) the wooden sword given to a gladiator to symbolize his permanent discharge from any further obligation to fight

secutor (Latin) the type of gladiator, armed with a short sword, who is trained to fight a *retiarius*

Sefer Torah (Hebrew) literally Book of the *Torah*, a handwritten copy of the *Torah*

Septuagint (Latin), literally the Translation of the Seventy, the Greek version of the Hebrew Bible

Shabbat (sing.), **Shabbatot** (pl.) (Hebrew) the Sabbath, the seventh day of the Jewish week, a day of rest observed from a few minutes before sunset on Friday to a few minutes after three stars appear in the sky on Saturday night

Sh'ma (Hebrew) the Hebrew prayer in which Jews declare their faith in the One G-d; the first word of that prayer, which means "Hear!"

spoliarium (Latin) the pit below the arena, where the bodies of slain beasts and gladiators are dragged to await mass burial

stoa (Greek) a long, low building of shops with a columned porch facing the center of the agora

Sukkot (Hebrew) the Festival of Booths, a seven-day Biblical holiday beginning on the fifteenth day of *Tishri*

Tishri (Hebrew) the first month of the civil year and the seventh month of the ecclesiastical year in the Hebrew calendar

Torah (Hebrew) the *Pentateuch*, the Five Books of Moses, the foundation of all Jewish legal and ethical precepts

tunica interior (Latin) a knee-length undergarment women wore under a chiton

Early Roman Emperors

Name	Reign
Augustus	27 BCE to 14 CE
Tiberius	14 CE to 37 CE
Caligula	37 CE to 41 CE
Claudius	41 CE to 54 CE

About the Author

Photograph by Michael Gold

June Trop (Zuckerman) is associate professor *emerita* of science education at the State University of New York at New Paltz. *The Deadliest Lie* is her first novel. She is working now on its sequel.